ETCHED IN STONE

A Stone Saga Novella

Book 3.5

DAKOTA WILLINK

Praise for The Stone Saga

"It's complex. It's dirty. And I relished every single wickedly hot detail." —**Not Your Moms Romance Blog**

"This read demanded to be heard. It screamed escape from the everyday and gave me that something extra I was looking for." — **The Book Junkie Reads**

"I was blown away! The angst, the passion, and the story line was amazing! I think I have a new favorite couple!" —**Once Upon A Romance Blog**

"Krys and Alexander story is addicting, and the chemistry is on fire! The rollercoaster of emotions was amazing, and the way these two brought in the drama was off the charts." —**Bookish Girl Reviews**

"I would gladly hand over my heart to Alexander Stone!" — **Crystal's Book World**

STAND ALONE BOOKS

The Sound of Silence (Dark Romantic Thriller)

Author Note

Dear Reader,

Thank you for choosing *Etched In Stone*. This novella is a spin off from *The Stone Saga*, a 5-book series that follows the same couple throughout.

Are you new to *The Stone Saga*? That's okay! This novella is considered book 3.5 in the series and can be read as a standalone.

Readers who wish to start at the beginning should read *Heart of Stone* first. You can expect a steamy romantic suspense with dark themes, including kidnapping, blackmail, death, and complicated family dynamics.

I hope you enjoy!

Dakota Willink

Etched In Stone

**A remote island. A ruthless man.
A honeymoon I'll never forget...**

Alexander promised me the dream.
He delivered something far more intoxicating.
On an untouched island of white sand and turquoise seas,
we vanished from the world. Every kiss was a claim, every
touch a command. My enigmatic husband ruled me with
equal parts tenderness and raw, unrelenting power—
setting my skin aflame and leaving me aching for more.
His obsession consumed me.
His control bound me.
And I surrendered—completely.

Chapter One

Krystina

I settled into the cushion of the jet's plush leather seat, the buttery-soft material yielding beneath me like an embrace. This wasn't just any aircraft—it was a flying sanctuary of indulgence, all rich mahogany panels gleaming under soft lighting and crystal fixtures that caught the late afternoon sun streaming through the windows. The cabin wrapped me in luxury, seeming to hold me as tenderly as my new husband as we jetted off to a world where only we existed.

My heart hadn't stopped fluttering since we said "I do" mere hours ago, each palpitation a reminder of the whirlwind of vows and kisses that had become my reality. The phantom weight of my wedding dress—now carefully packed away—still seemed to rustle around my ankles, replaced by the flowing material of my travel dress that Alexander had chosen for me. Even in this simple gesture, his attention to detail showed. The fabric was the exact shade of seafoam that showed off my sun-kissed skin, and made my brown eyes appear even richer than their usual warm chocolate color.

I stole a glance at Alexander, seated in regal repose next to me, and felt my breath catch as it always did when I truly looked at him. His dark hair was slightly tousled from running his fingers through it—a habit he had when deep in thought—and the late-day sun streaming through the jet's windows cast golden highlights across his strong jaw. He'd loosened his tie and unbuttoned the top button of his crisp white shirt, revealing just a hint of the chest I knew so intimately. His presence was both a soothing balm and a spark—he calmed the remnants of wedding day chaos that still buzzed in my veins while simultaneously igniting an electric anticipation for what lay ahead.

The magnitude of this new life still felt surreal.

Mrs. Alexander Stone.

The name played through my mind like a melody I couldn't stop humming. After everything we'd been through—the obstacles, the tragic circumstances, the moments when I thought I might lose him forever—here we were, husband and wife, embarking on our forever.

As if sensing the direction of my thoughts, Alexander turned from the newspaper he'd been reading and laid his hand on my thigh. His touch was immediate and electric, his thumb drawing slow, deliberate circles through the delicate fabric of my dress. The caress was possessive yet gentle, a silent claim that sent shivers racing up my spine. I leaned back into the plush headrest, allowing the sensation to wash over me, and closed my eyes to savor the intimate caress that promised so much more.

"I'm looking forward to three weeks of just us," he murmured, his voice dropping to that low timbre that never failed to make my pulse quicken. His fingers pressed slightly deeper, the heat of his palm burning through silk. "No interruptions, no business calls, no outside world. Just me worshipping every inch of your body whenever I want. Are you ready for that, angel?"

The endearment rolled off his tongue like honey, the way it always did, but somehow it felt different now. More permanent. More... mine. I opened my eyes to meet his sapphire gaze, finding reassurance there alongside a thrilling anticipation that made my core clench with want. Those eyes had seen me at my most vulnerable, had watched me break and rebuild, had witnessed every facet of who I was, and loved me anyway.

"More than ready," I responded, my voice a whisper laced with excitement. The words felt inadequate for the rush of emotion flooding through me. Ready didn't begin to cover the desperate need I had to lose myself in him, to explore this new dimension of our relationship without the weight of the outside world pressing down on us. "But I still don't know where we are going."

He smiled then, slow and devastating, the corners of his deep blue eyes crinkling with a secret that made him look younger and more carefree than I'd seen him in months.

"Patience, angel. I promise it's worth the wait."

Internally, I mused on the promise of our dream honeymoon, the allure heightened tenfold by the unknown destination. My imagination ran wild with possibilities—I envisioned pristine white sands and crystal-clear waters that shifted from turquoise to sapphire, or perhaps a European cityscape steeped in centuries of history and romance, cobblestone streets and intimate cafes where we could get lost in each other's over a bottle of wine. Or maybe a secluded mountain retreat where we could make love by firelight.

Wherever we were going, I was certain it would be special. Alexander's surprises were never anything short of extraordinary, each one more thoughtful and perfectly tailored to me than the last. He had a way of seeing straight into my soul and giving me things I didn't even know I wanted.

"Can you give me a hint?" I asked, unable to keep the pleading note from my voice. "Just a tiny one?"

Alexander shook his head, his smile widening as he watched my expression shift to mock disappointment.

"You need to trust me," he murmured, lifting my hand

to press a soft kiss to my wedding ring. The platinum band felt foreign and familiar all at once, a tangible reminder of the vows we'd exchanged.

Trust him.

The words echoed in my head, and I realized how completely, utterly true they were. I did trust him—with every fiber of my being and every beat of my heart. There had been a time when trust felt impossible, when my past had built walls so high I thought no one could scale them. But Alexander had torn down those barriers brick by brick, proving over and over that he was worthy of my faith, my love, my everything.

His thumb paused in its ministrations, pressing purposefully against my inner thigh in a way that drew a sharp gasp from my lips. Desire burned hot and bright in his eyes, transforming them from their usual cool blue to something molten and dangerous. Heat pooled low in my belly, my body responding to his touch with an urgency that still surprised me. Before I could see where that look would take us, before I could lean in and lose myself in the promise I saw there, the moment was punctuated by the smooth, powerful hum of the engines spinning to full power.

The private jet Alexander had commissioned was about to take off. Through the windows, I could see the ground crew moving with practiced efficiency, and my stomach fluttered with excitement that had nothing to do with flying and everything to do with the man beside me.

The force of acceleration pushed me back against the seat as we began our roll down the runway, the world outside becoming a blur of lights and movement until the wheels left the ground with barely a tremor. The jet climbed steeply, slicing through wisps of cotton-white clouds, carrying us away from everything familiar toward a mysterious paradise that existed somewhere beyond the horizon.

I leaned into Alexander, breathing in his familiar scent —expensive cologne mixed with something uniquely him that I could never quite name but would recognize anywhere. I was eager to begin our honeymoon properly, to experience the unending pleasures it would surely bring. Physical, yes, but also emotional. The chance to exist in our own private bubble, to learn new things about each other, to build a life with my husband without the constant intrusions of the outside world.

My husband.

Knowing he was mine sent a thrill through me. He was my compass, my anchor in every storm that had tried to tear us apart, my dominant guiding star in the darkest nights when I'd thought all hope was lost. The thrill of the unknown didn't unsettle me as it might have once. Instead, it filled me with excitement because he would be at my side through every moment of this adventure.

Always.

The warmth of Alexander's body pressed against me as his hand returned to my thigh, firm yet tender, each slow circle of his thumb sending ripples of anticipation through me that seemed to reach every nerve ending. His touch was a silent language all its own, one we'd developed over months of learning each other's bodies, needs, and darkest desires.

Time seemed to slow in the protection of the jet's hum, the steady drone of the engines creating a peaceful white noise that made the outside world feel very far away. My eyelids grew heavy, weighted down by more than just the gentle vibration of the aircraft. My wedding night with Alexander had been pure bliss—hours of worship and passion and whispered words of love—and neither of us had gotten more than an hour of actual sleep between the ceremony preparations and our early morning departure. The exhaustion was catching up with me now, my body finally allowing itself to relax completely for the first time in weeks.

I closed my eyes, welcoming the prospect of a peaceful nap wrapped in luxury and the security of Alexander's presence. As consciousness began to slip away, I felt him adjust beside me, his hand never leaving my leg, and I drifted off with a smile on my lips.

Chapter Two

Krystina

"Krystina." The sound of my name, spoken in that deep, familiar voice, pulled me slowly from the depths of dreamless sleep. Alexander's tone was gentle but insistent, designed to wake me without startling me. "You need to wake up, angel."

"Mmm..." I kept my eyes closed, not quite ready to leave the embrace of half-sleep, but I smiled and tilted my head in a way that had become second nature between us. The movement was subtle but deliberate, an invitation that granted him access to the delicate, sensitive skin just below my earlobe. I loved when he kissed me there—the spot that made me melt every single time—and he knew it.

From the Bluetooth speaker, "Adore You" by Harry

Styles drifted softly through the room, the dreamy melody and intimate lyrics wrapping around me. Each note seemed to echo the thrum of my heartbeat, every chord dripping with seduction.

Alexander's breath fanned over me, hot and inviting, making my pulse quicken. He leaned in closer, and I could feel the heat radiating from his body as his lips barely grazed the shell of my ear. When he spoke, his voice was rough with want, the words a sensual promise that made my toes curl in my shoes.

"I can't wait to see you wrapped in nothing but moonlight, spread out beneath me while I make you scream my name."

My eyes flew open as a shiver coursed through me, a delicious blend of nerves and excitement that started at my scalp and raced all the way down to my toes. Heat flooded my cheeks as Alexander's words painted images more vivid than any artist's canvas—a velvet night sky spangled with diamonds, the soft rustle of palm leaves in a gentle breeze, and the sensation of his hands exploring every contour of my moonlit flesh with patience and thoroughness that had become his signature.

"Is that where we're going?" I asked, my voice still husky from sleep. "The Caribbean?"

"Maybe," he teased, those sapphire eyes sparkling with mischief and reflecting a desire so palpable I could almost reach out and touch it. The corner of his mouth quirked up in that way that never failed to make my heart skip. "You still need to have patience, Mrs. Stone."

Mrs. Stone.

Hearing him say it sent another wave of giddy happiness through me.

"Patience is not one of my virtues," I reminded him, unconsciously leaning closer. "You know that better than anyone."

His hand tightened possessively on my thigh, and I saw the exact moment his control wavered. His pupils dilated, and he leaned forward as if to claim my lips, to show me exactly what he thought of my impatience. But before he could respond, before either of us could give in to the magnetic pull that never seemed to fade between us, the pilot's voice crackled through the cabin's intercom system.

"Crew members and passengers, we are beginning our descent into Montego Bay. Please prepare for landing and ensure your seatbelts are secure."

The spell broke, but the promise still lingered in the air between us, heavy and intoxicating. I straightened in my seat with reluctant obedience, peeling my gaze from Alexander's magnetic pull to look out the oval window beside me. Below us, an endless expanse of blue stretched out in every direction, the ocean's surface catching the golden light of late afternoon and throwing it back at us in a million glittering fragments. The water shifted from deep navy in the far distance to brilliant turquoise closer to shore, where I could just make out the outline of land emerging.

"Jamaica?" I asked, though the answer was already obvious. My heart did a little skip of excitement. I'd always wanted to visit the island, drawn by images of pristine beaches and crystal-clear water.

"I've reserved a private villa for us," Alexander confirmed, his business voice returning as he began folding the newspaper he'd been reading during my nap. But I caught the satisfied smile playing at his lips. "We'll stay for a few days to adjust and relax, then rendezvous with *The Lucy*. It gives us a period of rest and recharge, while allowing enough time for the crew to navigate her down the coast to meet us."

I raised an eyebrow, pleasantly surprised to hear we'd be spending time on Alexander's luxury yacht. *The Lucy* was his pride and joy, a stunning vessel that was more floating palace than boat. I loved being on the water—something about the endless horizon and the gentle rocking of the waves had always soothed my soul. It was why we'd chosen to get married on her decks in the first place, surrounded by our closest friends and family with the sunset painting the sky in shades of pink and gold.

"Where are we sailing?" I asked, unable to keep the excitement from my voice. The possibilities seemed endless.

"That, my beautiful wife, is still a surprise." He leaned in and kissed me softly on the lips, a gentle brush that somehow managed to convey both tenderness and barely restrained passion. "But I promise you'll love every minute of it."

My heart fluttered, marveling at this incredible life we were weaving together. Every thread seemed perfectly placed, every color more vibrant than the last. I was married to a man who'd move mountains to make me happy, who planned elaborate surprises just to see me smile, and who loved me with an intensity that still took my breath away.

The descent seemed to take forever and yet no time at all. I watched through the window as Jamaica grew larger and more detailed below us, revealing lush green mountains that rolled down to pristine beaches lapped by waters so clear I could see the coral reefs beneath the surface. The jet handled the approach with smooth precision, and I felt only the gentlest bump as the wheels touched down on the private airstrip.

When the engines finally wound down and the cabin door opened, a rush of warm, humid air greeted us, carrying the intoxicating scent of salt and tropical flowers. It hit me like a force, so different from the air-conditioned perfection of the jet, and I lifted my face to the sun for a moment, feeling some deep part of me unwind. I took a deep breath, letting the warm breeze fill my lungs. I pushed a strand of hair from my face, wishing for a rubber band to tie it back. As excited as I was to be here, many hair products were in my future if I had any hope of taming my curls in this humid air.

Alexander appeared at my side, his hand finding the small of my back in that protective gesture that had become so natural between us. Together, we stepped onto the sun-drenched tarmac of the small private airstrip.

A kaleidoscope of vivid blues and greens unfolded before my eyes in every direction. The Caribbean sky was an impossible shade of azure, so pure and brilliant it almost hurt to look at directly. It formed the perfect backdrop to the lush tropical foliage that framed the runway—towering palms that swayed in the breeze and flowering bushes bursting with color.

Alexander's arm slipped around my waist, pulling me closer to his side, and I felt his lips brush against my temple as he spoke words that seemed to sum up everything I was feeling.

"Welcome to our beginning, angel."

Chapter Three

Krystina

The tarmac was a carefully orchestrated ballet of efficiency. Despite the small size of the private airstrip, a team of uniformed porters moved with practiced precision, their movements fluid and purposeful as they retrieved our luggage from the jet's cargo hold. I watched in fascination as piece after piece emerged—more bags than I remembered packing. I suspected Alexander had added a few surprises of his own. The porters worked in comfortable silence, the only sounds the gentle wheeze of hydraulics and the distant call of tropical birds welcoming us to paradise.

Within minutes, our belongings were carefully arranged in the back of a pristine white van that gleamed under the Caribbean sun. The efficiency was impressive, but what struck me most was the evident respect these men had for my husband. They didn't just see him as another wealthy tourist—there was genuine deference in their movements, the kind that spoke of reputation.

"Mr. Stone," the head porter approached us, a distinguished man with silver at his temples and laugh lines that spoke of years spent in the sun. His accent carried the musical lilt of Jamaica, turning each word into something almost lyrical. "We will have your bags at the villa before you arrive, sir. You'll also find the refreshments our chef has prepared for your arrival— fresh fruit, some local specialties, and the Italian pastries Mrs. Stone favors."

My eyebrows shot up in surprise.

How did he know about my weakness for Italian pastries?

I glanced at Alexander, who was trying and failing to hide a self-satisfied smile. The man thought of everything.

"Is there anything else you need at this time?" the porter continued.

Alexander shook his head with the easy confidence of a man accustomed to having his wishes anticipated. "Thank you, Marcus. That will be all."

"Very well, sir." Marcus paused, turning toward a golf cart that waited nearby like a chariot ready to whisk us away to paradise. The vehicle was immaculate, its white paint job spotless and its seats cushioned in soft leather that looked far more comfortable than any golf cart had a right to be. He motioned toward it with obvious pride before pointing to a break in the foliage that surrounded the tarmac like a privacy screen. "As you requested, this cart is for your personal use during your stay. The navigation system is programmed on the dashboard, but you shouldn't need it to reach the villa. It's a pleasant five-minute ride down that path through the gardens until you reach the main house."

Alexander moved toward the golf cart with a confident stride that never failed to make my pulse quicken, his movements predatory and graceful all at once. He circled the vehicle with the same attention to detail he brought to everything else in his life, looking it over and running his hands along the seats as if ensuring the quality. Seeming satisfied with his inspection, he returned to my side, and I felt that familiar flutter in my chest at the way he looked at me—like I was the most precious thing in his world.

His hand found the small of my back once again, that possessive touch that had become as natural as breathing between us. Our eyes met as he helped me into the passenger seat, and in that fleeting exchange, a spark ignited between us that had nothing to do with the tropical heat.

His sapphire gaze held mine with an intensity that made my breath catch, whispering unspoken promises that made my core clench with anticipation. The corners of his mouth tilted upward in that knowing smile, and I felt a flush rise to my cheeks—partly from the blazing sun beating down on us, but mostly from the pure heat of his look.

"I hope that nap on the plane was enough to recharge you. I don't know how much rest you'll actually get over the next few days," he murmured, his voice dropping to that register that made my toes curl. There was a wicked gleam in his eyes. "I might have to rethink my plans, Mrs. Stone."

A fresh wave of giddy happiness washed through me. I'd never tire of hearing my new name on his lips, never stop feeling that little thrill of ownership and belonging that came with it.

"You won't hear any objection from me," I replied, surprised by the sultry tone of my own voice. The words came out as a mix of daring and devotion, mirroring the playful dance our fingers were performing as they intertwined on the seat between us. "Tell me about these plans."

"Patience, angel," he said, bringing our joined hands to his lips to press a soft kiss to my knuckles. "All will be revealed in due time."

The golf cart hummed to life beneath us with a gentle purr, and we began our journey down the winding path that would lead us to our temporary paradise. The route was flanked by the most exotic vegetation I'd ever seen. Ttowering palms that swayed hypnotically in the warm breeze. Flowering shrubs burst with colors so vibrant they seemed almost artificial—brilliant reds, shocking pinks, sunset oranges, and deep purples.

Again, I resisted the urge to pull my hair back from my face, knowing how much Alexander loved it when I left it loose. Right now, it was a cascade of unruly curls dancing in the breeze, and I could feel his eyes on me as the wind played with the strands.

"What are you thinking about, angel?" Alexander's voice was soft, intimate, as if he didn't want to disturb the peaceful spell that had settled over us as we drove.

"That it's beautiful here," I murmured, though the words felt inadequate to capture the wonder I was feeling. I breathed deeply, filling my lungs with air that seemed to carry magic in every molecule. The scent was intoxicating. Then I closed my eyes for a moment, letting the symphony of nature engulf me—the melody of exotic birds calling to each other from hidden perches, the gentle rustle of leaves, the rhythmic whisper of waves meeting shore. It was nature's own lullaby. "It's like something out of a dream."

"The best is yet to come," he promised, and something in his tone made me look at him more closely. There was anticipation there, excitement barely contained, as if he had a secret he was dying to share. He looked downright giddy, dropping his usual formal and controlled persona. It was so out of character for him, and seeing him like this brought a smile to my face.

The path curved gently through what could only be

described as an enchanted forest. With each turn, the vegetation seemed to grow lusher and more vibrant. The air grew thicker, more perfumed, until I felt almost drunk on the sensory overload.

When Alexander finally slowed the cart to a stop, I understood why he'd looked so pleased with himself. Nestled among a grove of palm trees was a structure that looked like something from a fairytale—a private villa just for us. But calling it a villa seemed almost insulting—this was a palace, an architectural masterpiece that seemed to have grown organically from the landscape itself, a harmonious blend of modern luxury and tropical charm. Its clean lines were softened by natural materials and an abundance of flowering vines that climbed the walls. Stone pathways meandered through carefully tended gardens where orchids bloomed, their delicate petals catching the sunlight that filtered through the palm canopy above.

Alexander stepped out of the cart, moving around to my side. He offered me his hand, and I took it, allowing him to help me down from the cart. As I started toward the entrance, I expected him to follow. Instead, he moved suddenly, sweeping me off my feet and into his arms with an ease that demonstrated his considerable strength.

I shrieked in surprise, my hands automatically going to his shoulders for stability as I found myself cradled against his chest. Looking up into his face, I saw a playful grin spreading across his chiseled features, transforming him from the serious businessman I'd married into something younger, more carefree.

"What in the world are you doing?" I asked, though I was laughing despite myself.

"Carrying you over the threshold," he said simply, as if it were the most obvious thing in the world.

The gesture was so unexpected—so unlike the Alexander I thought I knew. It took my breath away.

"I've seen the romantic side of you, but it's been a far cry from conventional. I didn't think you were the traditional romantic type."

"I'm not," he admitted, his grin widening as he adjusted his hold on me, making sure I was secure in his arms. "Think of this as a promise."

His strength was effortless, holding me as if I weighed nothing at all as he carried me up the stone pathway toward our temporary home.

"A promise?" I asked, genuinely curious.

"It's a promise to always lift you above the ordinary, to take you to places where only we exist, where the rest of the world can't touch us."

His words washed over me, leaving a trail of goosebumps in their wake. My heart swelled with so much love for this man that I thought it might burst from my chest. This was Alexander at his most vulnerable, most open, sharing a side of himself that he reserved only for me.

"Alex..." My voice came out fragile, trembling with the weight of emotions I couldn't quite put into words.

He paused at the threshold, looking down at me with such intensity that I felt exposed, seen in a way that was both thrilling and terrifying.

"I love you, Krystina Stone," he said simply.

Setting me down with exquisite care, as if I were made of the finest porcelain, Alexander brushed a stray curl from my face. His touch lingered, his fingertips tracing the line of my cheek with reverence. When I began to respond with my own words of affection, he hushed me.

"Shh." His finger moved to trace my jawline in a tender caress. "Save what you're thinking for later. Let's get settled first, and then we'll have all the time in the world to talk."

Chapter Four

Krystina

Alexander led me through the entrance and into a space that defied every expectation I'd had. The villa's open-air design was breathtaking, blurring the lines between the lavish comforts within and the wild, untamed beauty of the island beyond. Floor-to-ceiling openings invited the outside in, while gossamer curtains danced in the breeze that seemed to flow through every room. Sunlight streamed through the generous spaces, dancing across smooth stone floors and casting golden patterns on the walls. Delicate orchids perched like precious jewels in crystal vases, their exotic beauty adding splashes of color.

"Are you hungry?" Alexander asked, leading me through what appeared to be a living area toward the kitchen. "Marcus mentioned they'd prepared some things for us."

As if summoned by his words, my stomach chose that moment to growl audibly, reminding me that the excitement of our departure and the flight had left little time for proper meals.

"Starving, actually," I admitted with a laugh as I followed Alexander into a kitchen with gleaming marble countertops. Laid out before us was an elaborate spread— a feast for the senses that was almost too beautiful to disturb.

Fresh tropical fruits were artfully arranged on hand-crafted pottery. There were local specialties I couldn't immediately identify but that smelled heavenly. And, yes —a selection of Italian pastries that made my mouth water just looking at them.

Alexander selected a piece of mango and offered it to me. The fruit was impossibly sweet, bursting with flavor. Juice ran down my chin despite my best efforts, and Alexander was there immediately with a napkin, his touch gentle as he cleaned my face.

But the gesture was anything but innocent.

His thumb lingered at the corner of my mouth, his eyes darkening as he watched me with an intensity that made my breathing shallow.

"Later," he murmured, his voice rough with promise. "First, let's get the layout for the rest of the villa. Make no mistake, before we leave, I'll have taken you in every room of this place."

My stomach did a little flip, anxious to get to that part of our honeymoon, as he led me deeper into the intimate haven that was designed for seclusion and romance. Every detail spoke of careful planning, of someone who understood that luxury wasn't just about expensive things, but about creating experiences, moments, and memories. It was furnished with plush seating that beckoned invitingly, while French doors opened onto terraces that seemed to float among the treetops, offering glimpses of the ocean beyond. The lavishness around me was almost overwhelming, the kind of luxury I had only dreamed of before Alexander swept into my life and turned everything upside down.

One would think I'd be used to it by now, after months of being part of his world, but I wasn't sure I'd ever become completely accustomed to this level of lavishness. There was a part of me that still felt like a fraud—like someone playing dress-up in a life that belonged to someone else.

Low from hidden speakers throughout the villa, soft island music drifted through the air—a sultry blend of steel drums, distant congas, and a slow rhythm guitar that pulsed like a heartbeat. The melody was sensual and hypnotic, echoing the sounds of a tropical night, as if the ocean itself had set the rhythm for desire.

When we reached the primary bedroom, I couldn't

hold back my gasp of disbelief. The room was a fantasy made apparent. A massive canopy bed dominated the space, its frame crafted from what looked like driftwood polished to a soft gleam. Silk sheets in shades of cream and gold covered the king-sized mattress, whispering promises of the nights to come. Gossamer curtains surrounded the bed like a cloud, creating an intimate sanctuary within the larger room. The entire far wall was open to a private terrace that overlooked the ocean, where I could see an infinity pool that seemed to blend seamlessly with the horizon beyond.

"Wow... It's hard to believe this place it real."

"It's as real as it gets, angel," Alexander said, moving to stand behind me, his hands settling on my hips. "I wanted only the best for our honeymoon. You deserve nothing less."

Every detail of this place spoke of Alexander's thoughtful planning, his ability to anticipate needs I didn't even know I had. He knew how to touch my soul without saying a word, enveloping me in a love so profound that it seemed to resonate in the very air I breathed.

My throat tightened with emotion as I considered everything that had brought us to this moment. The past eight months had been a whirlwind—so much had happened during our intense, passionate courtship—if one would call it that. No one would ever consider Alexander and I conventional. There was the kidnapping that had left me hospitalized for weeks, and the trauma that had forced us both to confront our deepest fears. But the worst were the terrible secrets that had emerged about Alexander's family, decades-old lies that had shattered everything he thought he knew about his past.

We'd been tested in ways that might have destroyed other couples, but somehow, we'd emerged stronger and more committed—more certain that what we had was worth fighting for. The enormity of finally being here, finally being free to focus on just us without the weight of external demands, caused tears to sting the backs of my eyes. I shook my head, trying to organize my thoughts.

"No, Alex," I said, turning to face him. "This isn't just for me. After everything we've been through—the lies, the deception, the circumstances that threatened to tear us apart—now there are no more distractions. No more secrets to hold us back. Now is finally our time, and our time alone." I reached up to cup his face, feeling the slight roughness of stubble beneath my palms. "We deserve this. We've earned it."

"Krystina," Alexander said softly, his voice carrying a tenderness that never failed to undo me.

I turned to face him fully, my heart so full of love it felt like it might overflow. He placed his hands on either side of my neck, his touch both an anchor and a promise. Those hands—such a perfect contrast of strength and tenderness—had guided me through my darkest moments and lifted me to heights I'd never imagined possible.

"Alex," I responded, my voice barely above a whisper.

"I love you more than you can possibly know," he said, his voice a tender command that danced along my nerves and sent shivers cascading down my spine. "You are mine, and I am yours. Completely. Irrevocably."

His eyes, those pools of sapphire that I loved so much, held mine with a gaze so intense it seemed to peel back the layers of my soul, leaving me bare and wanting and completely his.

"Forever," I managed to say, though my voice was barely above a sigh, betraying the tremor of anticipation that had seized every nerve in my body.

A knowing smile tugged at the corners of his mouth, predatory and possessive and entirely Alexander. With deliberate slowness, he reached around to find the zipper of my dress, his knuckles brushing against my spine as he located the delicate tab. The metallic whisper of parting fabric was the sweetest symphony to my ears, each tooth of the zipper releasing its hold with a sound that seemed to echo in the charged air between us.

His fingers brushed against my newly exposed skin with a slow deliberation that bordered on exquisite torture, trailing fire in their wake as the dress loosened around me. I closed my eyes, surrendering completely to the meticulous undressing that was as much an exploration as it was a tease. Every touch was a word in the private language our bodies had developed, every caress a promise of the ecstasy I knew he would soon deliver.

A shiver, deep and uncontrollable, rippled down my spine, coiling at the base like a serpent preparing to strike. My skin felt hypersensitive, every nerve ending alive.

My dress fell away, waterfalling at my feet in a pool of seafoam. I stood before my husband in only the delicate lace of my bra and panties—pieces I'd chosen specifically for this moment, knowing he would appreciate the way the ivory complemented my skin.

Alexander's sapphire eyes, always so commanding and controlled, now smoldered with a hunger. They sent waves of liquid heat crashing through me. He looked at me not as a man simply appreciating his wife's body, but as an artist beholding a masterpiece, every curve and contour something to be adored and worshipped and claimed.

"Angel," he murmured, and the nickname sounded more like a sacred incantation falling from his lips. The air between us crackled with an electricity that drew us together with the inexorable pull of two opposing forces destined to become one.

Alexander moved closer, closing the small distance between us until his hard body was pressed against mine. The contrast was intoxicating—his fully clothed form against my near-nakedness. He cupped my face in his hands with a tenderness that contradicted his usual dominance, his thumb brushing across my cheek in a featherlight touch that somehow spoke louder than words.

It was a gesture of reverence, a silent vow that despite the intensity of our passion, despite the fire that burned between us, he would always handle me with care.

In that intimate embrace, with his hands framing my face and his body radiating heat against mine, the world outside our villa faded into complete insignificance. There was only him and me, only this moment, only the love that burned between us bright enough to eclipse everything else.

"Take me, Alex," I whispered, the words torn from somewhere deep in my soul. "Please."

The predatory gleam in his sapphire eyes intensified, becoming something primal and possessive that made my knees weak. It was a look that stripped away any pretense, leaving me bare and aching in its wake.

But instead of the immediate claim I expected, he surprised me.

"I will, angel. Tonight. I want you properly rested first." His voice was rough with restraint, as he struggled to control the desire I could see burning in his eyes. "For now, I want to see you in that little red bikini I bought for you. We'll go to the beach, relax for the afternoon. Or perhaps we can stay here and enjoy the infinity pool. Naked. Either way, I plan to take my time rubbing oil on every inch of your body."

My stomach tightened at the thought, heat pooling low in my belly at the images his words conjured.

"Every inch?" I asked, my voice breathless.

Alexander's hand moved with deliberate slowness, his fingers tracing a path from my collarbone down to cup my breast through the delicate lace of my bra. His thumb found my nipple, peaked from arousal, and circled it with maddening precision.

"Every," he confirmed, his voice a low growl of promise. "Inch."

Chapter Five

Alexander

The sun's golden rays caressed Krystina's bronzed skin as we lay on the pristine private beach off Montego Bay, the third day of what was proving to be the most perfect honeymoon I could have imagined. The stretch of sand and palm trees belonged exclusively to our villa—a crescent of powdered coral that curved between two rocky outcroppings like nature's own private amphitheater.

The days had been lazy in the best possible way, a deliberate contrast to the relentless pace of our lives back in New York. Here, time moved differently, measured not by the ticking of clocks or the buzz of smartphones, but by the rhythm of waves against shore and the arc of the sun across an impossibly blue sky. Our nights had been pure fire, passion unleashed without inhibition, but these quiet moments were equally precious.

I found myself studying my wife with the same intensity I brought to analyzing market trends, but with infinitely more pleasure. Krystina lay beside me on the oversized beach lounger we'd dragged into the perfect spot where the shade met the sun, her body barely contained by that tiny red bikini I'd chosen specifically for this moment. The vibrant color was striking against her sun-kissed skin, and I felt a surge of masculine satisfaction knowing I'd been right about how perfectly it would complement her curves and natural beauty.

My fingers traced lazy patterns across her coconut oil-slicked skin, unable to resist the magnetic pull of touching her. Marriage hadn't dimmed my need for physical contact with her—if anything, it had intensified it. The knowledge that she was mine, wholly and legally, had awakened something primitive in me that demanded constant confirmation of our connection.

God, she's breathtaking.

Even relaxed and drowsy from the heat, there was an elegance to her that never failed to stop me in my tracks. I'd been with beautiful women before, but none had ever affected me the way Krystina did. She was more than beautiful—she was luminous, radiant in a way that seemed to come from within.

"For the past three days, I don't think more than five minutes have passed without you touching me," Krystina observed, her voice lazy with contentment but tinged with amusement. She turned her head to look at me, those chocolate brown eyes sparkling with mischief that always made my pulse quicken. "You just can't keep your hands to yourself, can you?"

I smirked, continuing my sensual exploration of the curve where her waist met her hip. I allowed my finger to dip under her bikini line, teasing.

"I have three weeks to make up for all the days before the wedding when we couldn't touch because of propriety and schedules. Besides, you really can't blame me. You're beautiful. I can't help but want to touch you."

"Flatterer." She laughed, the sound like music carried on the ocean breeze. It was one of my favorite sounds in the world—pure, unguarded joy that seemed to bubble up from her very soul.

When Krystina moved to swat my hand away playfully, I was quicker. I pulled her flush against me, reveling in the feel of her soft skin against mine, warm from the sun and slick with the coconut oil I'd spent a considerable amount of time applying earlier.

"You love it," I murmured against her ear, my voice dropping to that register that I knew affected her. The scent of her hair—coconut and something uniquely Krystina—filled my senses.

I felt a delicious shiver run through her body, and I smiled with satisfaction. Even after months together, I could still affect her with just my voice, just my touch. It was a power I would never take for granted.

"Maybe," she conceded with a grin that was part innocent, part seductive, and completely irresistible.

The ocean stretched endlessly before us. Waves rolled in with hypnotic regularity, each one carrying foam that sparkled like scattered diamonds before dissolving into the sand. The sound was nature's own meditation, a constant whisper that seemed to wash away the stress and tension I'd carried for years without even realizing it.

"I never imagined retirement could feel like this," I mused, my fingers tangling in her salt-dampened curls.

Krystina propped herself up on one elbow, studying my face with those perceptive eyes.

"Retirement?"

"Temporary retirement for a few weeks—away from the chaos, the constant demands, the feeling that every moment has to be productive or profitable," I clarified. Even as I said it, I found myself questioning whether I wanted it to be temporary at all. I had enough money. We could retire now and never lack for anything. I gestured toward the pristine beach and the complete absence of anything resembling the corporate world. "When was the last time you saw me go more than an hour without checking my phone?"

"I can't remember," she admitted, her expression thoughtful. "You haven't mentioned Stone Enterprise since we left New York."

The realization was startling. Back home, my company was everything—the first thing I thought about when I woke up and the last thing on my mind before sleep. I'd built it from the ground up, transforming a relatively small real-estate investment into a global empire. It was my identity, my purpose, and my legacy.

Until I met Krystina—my angel.

With her warm and pliant in my arms, and the Caribbean sun warming my skin, I found I could barely summon the energy to care about quarterly reports or property acquisitions.

"Maybe that's what love does," I said, surprised by the philosophical turn of my own thoughts. "Makes you realize there's more to life than profit margins and market dominance."

"Look at you, getting all deep and introspective," Krystina teased, but there was tenderness in her voice. "I like this side of you. Relaxed Alexander is very appealing."

"Just appealing?" I asked, raising an eyebrow in mock offense.

"Devastatingly handsome," she corrected with a laugh. "Irresistibly charming. Dangerously attractive."

"Better," I said with satisfaction, pulling her closer.

I trailed kisses along her jaw, tasting salt and sunscreen. My mind wandered to last night in the villa, when I'd been buried deep inside her velvet heat under starlit skies. I wanted her again, right here on this secluded beach. I found myself thinking about our next destination. The private island I'd arranged for the second part of our honeymoon was even more secluded than this slice of paradise, a place where we truly would be the only souls for miles.

"What's going on in that head of yours, Mr. Stone?" Krystina's teasing voice broke through my fiery thoughts. "You have that look you get when you're planning something."

I met her gaze, seeing my desire reflected.

"Thinking about last night." My hand skimmed her thigh, inching higher. "And imagining all the ways I plan to worship your body later."

Her breath hitched. "Is that a promise?"

"Oh yes," I growled softly. "One I fully intend to keep."

A surge of possessiveness washed over me as I looked into Krystina's eyes. My gaze darkened with desire, and I felt a primal urge stirring deep within. With its raw beauty and isolation, this island seemed to awaken something wild and untamed inside me.

"You're mine," I whispered, my voice low and husky.

Krystina's eyes widened slightly, her pupils dilating.

"Alexander..." she breathed, her voice heavy with arousal.

I struggled internally with the intensity of her gaze. We were on a private beach, but a stranger walking the shoreline occasionally passed by. Part of me wanted to claim her, to mark her as my own, even if it meant being seen by anyone who might pass by. But I had to be careful.

Paparazzi could be anywhere, and her body deserved reverence in the privacy of our bedroom—not splashed all over the front page of a tabloid.

I leaned in, my lips finding that sensitive spot on Krystina's neck that always made her quake with need. My hands roamed her body, cupping her breasts through the thin fabric of her bikini top. I teased her nipples with my thumbs, feeling them harden beneath my touch.

"Oh..." she sighed softly. The sound made my already stiff cock impossibly harder.

"Holy hell, angel," I groaned. "Do you have any idea what you do to me?"

She arched into my touch, her breath coming faster.

"Show me," she challenged, her voice thick with longing.

"Oh, I intend to. Again and again."

I captured her mouth in a searing kiss, deliberately domineering. I pushed my tongue past her parted lips, tasting her with gentle flicks. Our tongues danced, all-consuming, as one hand moved possessively up and down her back while the other continued to work her nipple.

Pulling back, I glanced around. Confident that we were completely alone, I pulled a towel over her and shoved down the fabric of her bikini. When I captured a taut peak between my teeth, Krystina gasped.

"Alex! Wait. Someone might see us."

"Nobody is around, and if they are, I have you covered," I growled, sucking her nipple in long pulls.

Suddenly, she propped herself up on one elbow, her brown eyes sparkling with mischief as she pushed me away. "Do you know what we should do?"

"Fuck right here on the beach?" I suggested, even though I would never do any such thing. At least not here. It was too risky.

"Be serious, Alex."

"I am."

She pressed her lips together, adjusted her bikini back into place, and then pointed toward the ocean.

"We should go for a swim." She jumped to her feet, stretching muscles that had grown pleasantly lazy in the heat before reaching down to tug at my hand. "Come on, Mr. CEO. It's time for you to let loose a little more."

She tried to pull me upright despite the obvious disparity in our strength. I couldn't help but laugh at her determination.

"I thought I was doing just fine a moment ago."

"Oh, you were getting there," she said with mock seriousness. "But I think you could use a little more work. When was the last time you did something spontaneous? Something completely unplanned and maybe a little reckless?"

The question gave me pause. In my world, spontaneity was a luxury I couldn't afford. Every decision was calculated, every move strategic. The idea of acting without careful consideration went against every instinct I'd developed as a businessman.

But looking at Krystina, flushed with sun and happiness and completely at ease in her beauty, I felt something shift inside me. Maybe it was time I learned to act on impulse rather than analysis.

Taking advantage of my superior strength, I pulled her back against my chest, enjoying the way she fit perfectly against me despite her efforts to escape.

"Is this spontaneous enough for you?"

She struggled against me, laughing as she tried to break free from my hold. "Getting warmer, but I think you can do better."

"Oh, can I?" I asked, my voice dropping to a dangerous register. "And what exactly did you have in mind?"

"Chase me," she said. "I'll give you a head start to catch me in the water."

I couldn't help but laugh.

She continued to pull my hand until I was standing. She turned to head toward the shoreline, but I stopped her again by pulling her to my chest. Leaning in, I began to kiss her once more. However, she was so slick with oil that she wiggled out of my grasp before I had a chance to deepen the kiss.

"Come on, Alex." She grinned, backing toward the shoreline. "Afraid of getting wet?"

"No. I'd just rather make you wet."

"You're insatiable."

"And you're a terrible sub asking for a spanking."

Krystina's laughter rang out, pure and joyous.

"Promises, promises," she teased, wiggling her hips enticingly as she retreated toward the water's edge.

I took a step forward, a predatory gleam in my eye. "You'd better start running, angel. Because when I catch you..."

She squealed in mock terror, turning to dash toward the inviting waters. I gave her a head start, admiring how her curves moved as she ran. Then, with a grin, I sprinted after her, ready to show her exactly what would happen when she challenged me.

Chapter Six

Alexander

Krystina reached the water's edge just ahead of me, the waves lapping at her ankles as she turned to gauge my progress. Her laughter rang out across the empty beach, pure and joyous, and I felt my heart clench with love so intense it was almost painful.

As we plunged into the water, droplets splashed around us, catching the sunlight and transforming into a dazzling array of miniature rainbows. Krystina laughed again, playfully splashing water in my direction.

"Oh, you're asking for it now," I growled, lunging toward her.

She darted away, her lithe form cutting through the water with grace. "Catch me if you can!"

I chuckled, the sound rumbling from my chest as I chased her. The cool water caressed my skin, a refreshing relief from the tropical heat. As I closed the distance between us, I couldn't help but marvel once again at Krystina's beauty. Her brown curls, now slick with water, framed her face perfectly, and her eyes sparkled with humor.

When I reached her, I wrapped my arms around her waist, pulling her back to my chest.

"Gotcha," I murmured, my lips brushing her ear.

"Mmm, so you have," she purred, turning in my arms to face me. "What are you going to do with me now?"

The playfulness in her tone reignited the fire within me.

"Oh, I have a few ideas," I replied, my voice husky with desire.

We lingered in the water, bodies entwined, exploring and teasing. I pressed my hand between her legs, taking full advantage of the water's privacy as I sought her hard bundle of nerves beneath the protection of her bikini.

Her breath caught, and she angled her pelvis up to meet the pressure of my fingers. I buried my face into her neck and breathed in deeply. Peppering kisses along her hairline, I moved over to her ear and bit her lobe. She threw back her head, welcoming me to take more as my lips traveled down her neck. I was suddenly desperate, feeling as if it had been way too long since I'd had her.

She reached around, slipping a hand inside my shorts, and gripped my cock. When she began to stroke from base to tip, I groaned.

"Alex," she breathed. "I want you inside me."

If her words weren't enough to unravel me, her magical hands were.

I shifted positions, sliding a hand over her smooth belly and under the waistband of her bikini until I reached her wet slit. My forefinger circled her nub furiously, needing to get her off so that I could take her back to the villa and fuck her properly in a bed.

She continued stroking me, her grasp tightening around my cock as I plunged two fingers inside to stroke her walls.

The sound of distant laughter had me looking up. Far down the beach, but close enough to be heard, a couple with a small child entered the water.

Fuck.

Krystina and I were both panting and breathless, needing release. Reluctantly, I pulled away.

"There are people down the shore," I pointed out. "Let's go dry off. We can finish what we started here back at the villa."

Krystina removed her hand from my shorts and followed my gaze.

"Damn," she quietly hissed, that single word expressing a need that matched my own. Then suddenly, her expression shifted to something mischievous, and she grinned. "Race you back."

"You're on," I replied, not needing an excuse to hurry back to the villa.

We both struck out with strong, steady strokes. She was a better swimmer than I'd realized, her form efficient and graceful as she cut through the water. I could have easily outpaced her, but I found myself holding back, content to swim alongside her and watch the concentration on her face as she pushed herself to keep up. When we reached shore, we took off running back to the secluded area where we'd left our towels and chair.

I let her win.

Both breathing hard but exhilarated, Krystina turned to me with triumph shining in her eyes. "I think I won."

"I suppose you did. What's my penalty for losing?"

"Hmm," she said, placing a finger on her chin contemplatively. "You have to tell me one thing about yourself that I don't know. Something real."

The request caught me off guard. I was a private person by nature, someone who revealed information strategically and sparingly.

"There's unfinished business to attend to back at the villa. I'm pretty sure your wet pussy would agree. Can this wait until after?"

"Nope," she stated, planting her feet firmly in the sand.

Something about the way she looked at me, hopeful and open and completely without guile, made me want to give her what she asked for. It was either that or I was just desperate for the release I'd been denied just moments before.

"When I was eight," I heard myself saying, "I wanted to run away and join a sailing crew."

"Like a pirate," she teased.

"Yeah, a lot like a pirate. I'd read about these expeditions that went around the world, and I was convinced that was the life for me—away from the hell I was living in. I even packed a bag and made it to the marina before my grandfather found me."

Krystina's eyes widened with surprise. "And then what happened?"

"He didn't lecture me or punish me," I continued, surprised by how vivid the memory still was. I'd forgotten about it up until that moment. "He just sat down on the dock next to me and asked what I was running from. And when I told him I just wanted to get away from everything, he said he understood. But then he reminded me that I wouldn't be able to look out for Justine if I did that. His reminder about my sister was all I needed to go back. He told me that someday, when I was older, we'd take a boat trip together. Just the two of us. But then he died before that happened and..."

The memory brought with it a familiar ache of loss

and a promise of another thing that was robbed from my childhood.

"That's why you bought *The Lucy*," Krystina said softly, understanding flickering in her eyes.

"Perhaps," I admitted. "I never really thought of it like that, but maybe it had been a subconscious decision."

She moved closer to me, close enough that I could see tiny flecks of deep gold in her brown eyes. "Thank you for telling me that. Now, I want you to promise me something."

"Anything."

"Promise me that no matter how crazy things get when we go back to New York, you'll remember that you're not just Alexander Stone, CEO. You're also my husband, the man who chased me into the ocean and told me stories about running away to be a pirate."

"I promise," I said, and meant it with every fiber of my being. "Come on, angel. Let's get back to the villa."

As we crossed the sand, Krystina walked slightly ahead of me. Still wet from our dip in the ocean, I enjoyed watching the water cascade down her curves—and so did the male jogger headed our way. My eyes narrowed at how he looked at her—my wife.

My gaze shifted back to Krystina. Her bikini clung to her body, leaving little to the imagination, and I felt a primal surge of possessiveness. Jealousy crashed over me, and an overwhelming need to protect my wife.

Jogging to catch up with her, I quickly draped a towel

around her shoulders, annoyed at myself for being so irrational. I knew the jogger was harmless.

"I can't wait until we get someplace more private," I mumbled.

"What's wrong?" she asked, obviously picking up on my surly tone.

"I just don't like it when other men gawk at you. It makes me crazy."

Confusion came over her face until she looked over my shoulder and spotted the runner just down the beach.

Smiling, she stopped and turned toward me, pressing a finger to my chest. "Jealous?"

"Don't push me, angel. When I bought that bikini for you, I'd intended it for the next stop on our honeymoon."

Krystina looked up at me through her thick lashes, a coy smile on her lips. "Are you going to tell me where we are going finally?"

I leaned in, my voice dropping to a low rumble. "A private island. We'll be the only two souls present, and I'll be able to enjoy my view of you from wherever I want without worrying about bystanders."

Krystina's eyes softened, and she leaned in, her lips brushing mine in a tender kiss.

"I love you, Alexander Stone," she whispered. "Even when you're acting like a possessive neanderthal."

"You haven't seen anything yet. I've been looking at you mostly naked for the better part of the day, and the need to explore every inch of your body is starting to take over. You'll be screaming my name within the hour," I promised, my words dripping with intent.

"Alex..." My name was a breath on her lips, and I couldn't help but imagine all the ways to pleasure her later.

I offered her my hand. "Let's go. I want you begging and trembling beneath me."

When we reached the villa, the air between us crackled with unspoken desire. I guided Krystina to the door, my hand on her lower back. My fingertips grazed the soft skin just above her bikini bottoms. She shivered at my touch, and I felt a primal surge of satisfaction.

"After you, angel," I murmured once the door swung open.

Krystina stepped inside, and I followed, closing the door behind us. The soft click of the latch felt like a starting gun, signaling the beginning of the marathon I had planned for tonight.

The low sun bathed the villa's interior in a golden glow, giving everything a dreamlike quality. My eyes were drawn to Krystina, her sun-kissed skin radiant in this light. When she turned to face me, I captured her lips, pouring all my pent-up desire into the kiss.

"God, I want you," I hummed against her, my hands roaming her curves greedily.

She responded eagerly, her fingers threading through my hair and pressing herself closer. The taste of her, mixed with the lingering salt from the ocean, was intoxicating. When she pulled away, we were both panting.

"Can you give me a few minutes? I just want to shower quickly to get the oil and sand off me."

"I'll join you," I murmured.

"Mmm... as enticing as that sounds, I must do girly things, too. I'll meet you in the bedroom."

I smirked but didn't comment about whatever girly things she needed to do. I could allow her a bit of privacy if that's what she required.

"Go ahead. I'll shower in the guest bath. Take all the time you need, angel—but don't be too long."

She stepped back slightly, her brown eyes dancing with mischief. "I won't be. I wouldn't dare keep the controlling Mr. Stone waiting."

The use of my formal name ignited something primal within me. I gripped her hips firmly, backing her up against the nearest wall.

"Is that what you want?" I asked, my voice low and commanding. "For me to take control?"

I pressed my hard cock against her. Krystina's breath hitched, her pupils dilating with arousal.

"Yes," she whispered. "It's what I always want. I want all of you—every dominant, possessive inch. I'm yours. Completely."

The promise in her words, the trust she consistently placed in me, was overwhelming. I captured her lips again, this kiss deeper, more consuming. My hands slid down to her thighs, and in one smooth motion, I lifted her, pinning her between my body and the wall.

Krystina wrapped her legs around my waist, looping her arms around my neck. I trailed kisses along her jaw, down her neck, reveling in every soft sigh and moan she made.

"I need to touch you. Everywhere."

"Let me shower first, I'm—"

Covering her mouth with mine, I didn't allow her to say anything else. With one arm banded around her waist, I used my free hand to greedily push aside the tiny triangles of her bikini top, allowing her breasts to spill free. Lowering my head, I captured a nipple between my teeth. She gripped my shoulders with both hands and arched, encouraging me to take my fill. When I began to circle my tongue over her supple areola, she moaned, and I nearly came on the spot. There was no doubt that Krystina and I would be explosive once we finally made it to a bed.

"Say my name. I want to hear my name on your lips," I told her, speaking the words into her cleavage as I moved my mouth between each tit, refusing to let one get more attention than the other.

"Alex."

"Your body is mine."

"Yes!" She gasped out the word, her desperation evident. "My body is yours."

Her hands snaked around the base of my neck as she

arched her back, searching for more, and I was determined to give her exactly that. Sliding my hand from her breast, I pulled the tied strings at her hips, allowing her bikini bottom to fall free. When my fingers connected with her wet slit, we both gasped.

"God, you're so fucking wet," I murmured. I circled her hard clit for a moment, then drove a finger inside her heated well. Her breath hitched, and her hips pushed upward, taking what I offered with fevered urgency. I increased my tempo, building momentum until she was whimpering with need. She was driving me fucking wild.

"Come for me, angel. I want you to come on my hand."

She kissed me frantically, and my fingers thrust deeper to massage and stroke her walls, only pulling out to trace wet circles around her throbbing nub. I felt her body tense, and her shallow breathing began to come faster.

She was close.

I quickened the pace, flexing my fingers with more urgency until I could feel the slight tremors of her building orgasm. I wanted to give her this—to make her think about my touch while she was in the shower. To make her desperate to feel my cock buried inside her.

When I knew she was almost there, I tore my mouth from hers to see her face. I wanted to watch her as she fell apart. Her eyes grew wide, then snapped closed, and I was rewarded with her cry of pleasure as she shattered against my palm. Her ecstasy faded to enfolding aftershocks, and her eyes slowly fluttered open.

Once her breathing began to regulate, she clasped my face between her hands and pulled my head down to hers for a low, languid kiss. When she pulled away, there was no mistaking the glowing embers in her gaze.

"That was just a taste, angel. Before the night is over, you'll be begging for me to stop."

Chapter Seven

Alexander

I took Krystina's hand and stepped out of our private villa into the warm sunshine. The morning air was already thick with humidity and the promise of another perfect day in paradise. I interlaced my fingers with hers, savoring the softness of her skin and the feel of her wedding ring— a symbol to everyone that this incredible woman was now mine.

It was day five of our honeymoon, and I had planned something different for today. Instead of lounging on our private beach or the villa's terrace, the vibrant culture of Jamaican local life pulsed just beyond our luxurious bubble, and I wanted to show some of it to Krystina.

"Where are we going?" she asked, her eyes sparkling

with curiosity as our driver navigated the winding coastal road toward Montego Bay.

"A local market," I replied, enjoying the way her face lit up with excitement. "I thought you might enjoy seeing the real Jamaica, not just the private resort version."

"Really?" Her surprise was evident. "That sounds very domestic...and crowded. And unlike you."

I laughed, understanding her confusion. There was a time when I would have preferred controlled environments that could be managed and predicted. But something about being married to Krystina was changing me in ways I was still discovering.

"Maybe that's the point," I said, bringing her hand to my lips to press a gentle kiss to her knuckles. "You make me want to try new things, to see the world through your eyes."

As we walked hand-in-hand through the colorful, bustling streets of Montego Bay's central market, I found myself captivated not just by the sights and sounds around us, but by Krystina's reactions. She turned to me frequently with that playful smile I adored, her eyes sparkling with excitement.

"Everything is so lively here," she marveled, gesturing around us. The market was a sensory feast unlike anything in our usual world. Stalls lined narrow cobblestone streets in a maze of commerce and culture that had probably existed in some form for generations. Rainbow-colored sarongs fluttered in the warm breeze, while vendors called out in lilting jargon that turned even the most mundane sales pitch into music. Tables groaned under the weight of handwoven baskets, intricate wood carvings, and paintings that seemed to capture the very essence of the island's spirit.

"It is," I agreed, pulling her a little closer to my side as a group of boisterous tourists pushed past us. The protective gesture was automatic, but I found myself studying the effortless way she navigated the chaos. I lifted our joined hands to press a tender kiss to her knuckles. Her brown eyes met mine, radiating pure happiness and affection.

My heart swelled with love for her. A part of me still didn't believe she was real. Devils weren't worthy of angels, yet here she was.

The mouthwatering scent of jerk chicken sizzling on a nearby grill mixed tantalizingly with the sweet fragrance of ripe mangoes and papayas. Lively beats of steel drum music filled the air as locals and tourists chattered and bartered animatedly. The rhythm was infectious—bright percussion laced with the smooth undertone of a bass guitar, punctuated by the occasional trill of a flute. It rose and fell like the tide, sensual and playful. The island's music wasn't just background noise—it was life itself, weaving its pulse into the very culture of this place.

Krystina paused before a stall where an older woman sat surrounded by handmade jewelry. The vendor, her skin the color of rich coffee and lined with the wisdom of decades, looked up from her work with a smile that transformed her entire face.

"Good morning, beautiful lady," she said in heavily accented English. "You looking for something special for your honeymoon, yes?"

Krystina blushed, her hand instinctively going to the rings on her left hand. "How did you know?"

The woman laughed, a sound like wind chimes. "Child, love like yours, it shines so bright even a blind man could see it. You both glow like you swallowed sunshine."

"See anything you like?" I asked as Krystina examined a collection of delicate seashell jewelry, each piece handmade with painstaking attention to detail.

"So many beautiful things," she mused. Turning to me with a coy smile, she added, "Present company included."

I smirked and wound an arm around her waist, tugging her flush against me despite the public setting. The playful banter we'd shared since starting our honeymoon was unlike our usual dynamic, yet it felt completely natural. Marriage had given us a new kind of freedom, a sense of security that allowed me to explore different facets of our relationship that had once been foreign.

"Likewise, angel." Then I leaned down to whisper so only she could hear, "I plan to show you how much I admire your beauty later."

Krystina trembled slightly, her eyes darkening with

desire as she murmured, "I think you already did that last night. And the night before, and the night before that."

"And I'll do it again tonight."

"You have good taste, sister," the jewelry vendor said approvingly, interrupting our private moment. "Your man, he looks at you like you are made of starlight."

"What would you recommend?" I asked the woman, genuinely curious about her perspective. "Perhaps something that captures the culture of Jamaica?"

Her eyes lit up as she reached beneath her table, emerging with a small wooden box that looked very old.

"This one," she said, lifting out a bracelet made of what appeared to be sea glass and tiny shells, connected by fine silver wire. "It is made from glass the ocean gave back to us, and shells from the deepest waters. It carries the blessing of the sea goddess, protection for love that crosses many waters."

Krystina smiled softly, and I could see the piece had spoken to her in some way.

"It's perfect," she whispered.

As I paid for the bracelet—paying far more than the asking price because the woman's craftsmanship deserved it—I found myself thinking about the symbolism she'd mentioned.

Love that crosses many waters.

Krystina and I had certainly weathered our share of storms.

As we continued through the market, Krystina's

enthusiasm proved infectious. She stopped to admire hand-painted masks, asked vendors about their techniques, and even convinced me to try a piece of sugarcane that a farmer pressed into our hands.

"When I was little," Krystina said as we paused near a fountain where local children were playing. "I dreamt about places like this. Somewhere warm and colorful and alive, where people smiled for no reason except that they were happy to be alive."

"And now here you are," I murmured, watching her profile as she observed the splashing children with a wistful expression.

"Yeah, here I am," she said with a slight shrug. "Before Frank, my mother and I had so little when I was younger. Daydreaming about tropical paradises had always seemed like just that—a dream."

"Well," I said, pulling her closer, "now you don't have to dream about it. We can go anywhere you want, see anything that calls to you."

She turned to look at me fully, and I saw something deep and complicated in her brown eyes.

"That's still hard for me to believe sometimes. That this is real, that I'm allowed to have this much happiness."

"You're not just allowed to have it," I said firmly. "You deserve it. You deserve everything good this world has to offer."

A group of local musicians had gathered near the fountain, their impromptu concert drawing a small crowd.

The music was hypnotic, complex rhythms layered over melodies that seemed to tell stories of heartbreak and hope, loss and redemption. Without thinking, I found myself swaying slightly to the beat.

"Dance with me," Krystina said suddenly, holding out her hand.

"Here?" I asked, looking around at the crowd of strangers.

"Here," she confirmed, her eyes sparkling with mischief. "Come on, remember what we talked about yesterday? About being spontaneous?"

Before I could overthink it, I took her hand and pulled her into a dance, moving to the infectious rhythm while tourists and locals alike smiled and clapped around us. Krystina laughed with pure joy, her head thrown back, and I thought this might be the most perfect moment of my entire life. It seemed as though I were having a lot of those lately.

As the song ended and we made our way to a quieter section of the market, I found myself studying my wife once more. I recalled our first date—even if I hadn't realized that was what it was at the time. Krystina and I had walked through Washington Square Park, where she'd found joy in a woman feeding squirrels and a young boy playing the guitar under a tree. She had this gift for finding magic in ordinary moments, for transforming even a simple market visit into something extraordinary.

"Thank you," I said as we paused to admire a display of local artwork.

"For what?"

"For teaching me how to live in the moment instead of constantly planning the next move."

She smiled, but there was something thoughtful in her expression.

"Speaking of the future," she said carefully, "what do you see for us? I mean, beyond the honeymoon, beyond settling into married life. What do you want our life to look like five years from now? Ten years?"

The question caught me off guard. We'd talked about many things during our relationship, but we'd never really discussed long-term plans beyond the wedding itself.

"I see us happy," I said slowly, trying to organize thoughts I'd never fully articulated. "I see a life where we never lose this connection we have, where we keep discovering new things about each other."

"And family?" she asked, her voice carefully neutral. "Do you ever think about children?"

The word hit me like a cold wind despite the tropical heat.

Children.

It was a topic I'd successfully avoided thinking about for years, one that brought up complicated feelings I wasn't sure I was ready to examine. Krystina had only mentioned having kids once—at our wedding reception.

But it had been said in passing, having never come up before that.

"I..." I started, then stopped, unsure how to voice the tangle of emotions the question provoked.

Krystina must have sensed my discomfort because she quickly backtracked. "I'm sorry, I didn't mean to put you on the spot. It's just something I've been thinking about. Being around you, seeing how protective and caring you are, makes me wonder what kind of father you'd be."

"Krystina, it's not that I don't want to talk about it. It's just... complicated for me."

"Because of your own father?"

The perceptiveness of her question shouldn't have surprised me, but it did.

"Partly," I admitted. "I'm not sure I have a clear picture of what fatherhood is supposed to look like. The way I was raised..."

She squeezed my hand encouragingly. "But you've grown beyond that."

"Have I?" I asked, genuinely uncertain. "Sometimes, I look at how much I value control, and I wonder if I'm capable of bringing another human into a world of uncertainty. I can provide financially, but I don't know if I can give emotionally simply because I don't know how."

"Alex," Krystina said softly. "The fact that you're even worried about it tells me you'd be nothing like that. You're the most devoted, attentive man I've ever known.

Controlling, yes. But good. You've spent our entire honeymoon focused completely on me—on us."

"That's different," I protested. "You're my wife. I chose you, and I am committed to you. A child would be..."

"What?" she prompted when I trailed off.

"Vulnerable," I finished quietly. "Completely dependent on me not to screw up their life the way mine was screwed up."

We stood in silence for a moment, watching the bustling life of the market continue around us. Finally, Krystina spoke again.

"I think about it sometimes," she said. "What it might be like to give a child all the love and stability you never had. To create the kind of family where children feel safe and valued and wanted."

The wistfulness in her voice made my chest tight.

"You'd be an incredible mother," I said, and meant it completely.

"And you'd be an amazing father," she replied with quiet conviction. "I know how it feels to be loved by you. You love completely. You could never be absent or neglectful. If anything, I think you'd be overprotective of a child."

A reluctant smile tugged at my lips. "You could count on that."

"We don't have to decide anything now," she said, her tone light but understanding. "I'm not ready to jump into parenthood. I want to be us for a while. I just wanted to know if it were something you'd be open to down the road."

"It is now," I admitted. "You've made a lot of things seem possible that I never thought I wanted."

The conversation had taken an unexpectedly serious turn. These were the kinds of discussions married couples needed to have. Deep explorations of hopes and fears that built the foundation for a lifetime together were normal. It felt right, but made me uncomfortable at the same time. The idea of children was terrifying and appealing in equal measure.

"So," I said, shifting to lighter territory. "Ready to see what other treasures this market has to offer?"

"Absolutely," she said, her smile bright and grateful. "And then maybe you can tell me more about this mysterious destination we're sailing to tomorrow."

"Nice try," I laughed. "But that's still a surprise."

"I'm assuming we'll still be in hot weather," she prompted, fishing for clues.

"Definitely hot," I said, enjoying the way her eyes lit up with curiosity. "Think tropical paradise, but even more secluded than where we are now."

"You mentioned a private island. Is it more secluded than our private villa?"

"Much more," I confirmed. "Picture the most beautiful, untouched beach you can imagine, with crystal clear water and absolutely no one around for miles."

Her breath caught slightly. "How is that possible?"

"I have resourceful friends. When I want true privacy, I know how to get it."

Tomorrow, we were set to board *The Lucy*, cruising toward Enchanted Isle, the private oasis I'd arranged. The undeveloped land mass was a recent purchase by a friend who owed me a favor. No building structures were on the island, nor was there electricity or plumbing. Krystina and I would utilize *The Lucy* for modern amenities, only returning to civilized land for provisions and refueling. The island was nothing but palm trees on a white sandy beach. There would be no other people—and no worries about the press. I'd been careful with our honeymoon planning, but I'd feel better knowing no intrusive paparazzi were lurking in the bushes. On Enchanted Isle, I could worship every inch of Krystina's luscious body whenever and wherever I pleased.

Krystina looked up at me curiously. "You seem lost in thought. What are you thinking about?"

"That I can't wait until we leave aboard *The Lucy* tomorrow. I'm anxious to have you all to myself."

Her eyes sparkled with excitement, but I also sensed a hint of apprehension. "I know we've only been away for five days, but time is flying by. I don't want our honeymoon to end."

A mischievous grin curled my lips. Pulling her around to the back of a shop stall, I pulled her against me and leaned in so only she could hear my words.

"Trust me, Krystina. We're just getting started. I've

only just begun inflicting torture on your body," I whispered against the shell of her ear.

Just as I'd intended, her breathing quickened, erasing her apprehension. With every breath she took, I could feel her mounting desire.

"Oh, really, sir?"

"I haven't tied you up yet."

"Hmm, no, you haven't."

"I want you bound and helpless—to own every inch of your body, including your ass. I haven't claimed that since you've become Mrs. Alexander Stone. I'll need to rectify that soon, angel. You'll be begging for my cock to take you there."

She sucked in a sharp breath, but her expression didn't waver. "Is that so?"

"Don't be coy, Krystina. I know you too well and know exactly how you like it. I can feel the way your nipples hardened at the suggestion."

Stepping away, I let her absorb my words. She pulled her arms up, attempting to hide her traitorous breasts. Desire pooled in her eyes, and it was all I could do not to take her back to the villa and fuck her senseless. But there would be time for that later.

Chuckling, I took her hand in mine. "Come on, angel. There's more to explore."

Chapter 8

Alexander

After perusing the market and purchasing a few souvenirs, we returned to the villa where we could get the privacy we craved. As our hired driver navigated the winding road, I kept one hand possessively on Krystina's thigh, my thumb tracing slow circles on her thigh. She'd grown quiet since our conversation about children, but I could read every nuance of her expression, every subtle shift in her breathing. After months of studying her, claiming her, making her mine, I thought I knew her better than she knew herself.

But I couldn't get a read on her now.

"Tell me what you're thinking," I commanded softly, my grip tightening slightly on her leg. It wasn't a request

—I wanted to dissect every thought that passed through her beautiful mind.

She turned to look at me, those chocolate brown eyes reflecting the golden light, but more importantly, reflecting the trust she'd placed entirely in my hands.

"I was just thinking about how different our conversations feel on this trip. Back in New York, we're always so focused on the immediate—work, schedules, and the next obligation. Arguing about your need for constant control," she added with a teasing wink. "But here, talking about our future, feels different than at home —we feel different. I don't know if it's because of where we are, or if it's because we're now officially married. But it's like I can dream with the realization that nothing is out of reach."

"What do you dream of?" I asked, bringing her hand to my mouth, pressing her skin to my lips to remind her who she belonged to. Every kiss was a brand, every touch a claim.

"Simple things, mostly. Like having Sunday morning breakfasts that last for hours because we have nowhere else to be. Or taking spontaneous trips to places we've never been, just because we saw a photograph that made us curious." She paused, and I could see her gathering courage to reveal more. "Or reviewing the blueprints for our future home—a sanctuary for both of us, with mutual respect but where you're always in control. I'd be safe and protected."

Her words stirred something primitive and possessive deep in my chest. The need to protect and provide for a woman who needed neither was real. To create a world where she could flourish was as fundamental to my nature as breathing.

"You'll have all of that," I said, my voice carrying the weight of absolute certainty. "I'll give you everything you've ever dreamed of and things you haven't even imagined yet. I'll always protect what's mine."

The way her pupils dilated at my words sent satisfaction coursing through me. She needed my strength, my control, as much as I needed her submission.

"I never knew I wanted to surrender control until I met you—even if I begrudgingly give it at times," she admitted, her voice barely above a whisper. "My whole life, I had to be strong, had to fight for everything. But with you..." She trailed off, searching for words.

"With me, you can let go," I finished for her, my hand moving to cup the back of her neck in a gesture that was both protective and possessive. "Your only job is to trust me."

The car rounded a curve, and suddenly our villa came into view. But I barely glanced at the structure—my attention was focused entirely on the woman beside me, on the way her breathing had quickened, on the flush spreading across her cheeks. She was responding to my dominance exactly as she was meant to.

A sultry Caribbean twilight descended, and a warm

breeze swirled around us, ruffling Krystina's curls as we stepped away from the car. My hand rested possessively on the small of her back as we walked, the heat of my touch seeping through the thin fabric of her sundress.

"Look at the sky," Krystina said, tilting her head back in that graceful way that exposed the elegant line of her throat. My mark wasn't visible there yet, but it would be. Soon.

I followed her gaze, but my attention was divided between the spectacular sunset and the way the colored light played across her skin. Everything about this moment—the isolation, the beauty, the woman at my side —reinforced my sense of ownership, of having claimed something rare and precious.

Most of the words we'd exchanged throughout the day were laden with sexual teasing and innuendo. Now, desire hung thick in the balmy air between us, and every nerve ending felt electrified. We barely made it through the villa's front door before I had her pressed up against the wall.

"I need to possess you completely," I growled, my voice taking on the authoritative edge that made her shiver. "Mind, body, and soul."

My mouth claimed hers in a hungry kiss, and my cock throbbed, already desperate for relief. Krystina wrapped her arms around my neck, surrendering entirely to me in a way that made me impossibly hard. When we finally came up for air, her eyes seared into mine, dark and full of need.

"Mrs. Stone," I whispered, gripping her waist possessively. "Come with me to the bedroom. I want to own your pleasure. Your pain. And every scream."

The way her eyes darkened at my words, the slight parting of her lips, told me everything I needed to know about how I affected her. She needed this as much as I did—needed to surrender control as much as I needed to take it.

"Mmm, yes. Show me," she purred, a wicked glint in her chocolate eyes.

The surrender in her voice, the complete trust in her gaze, sent electricity racing through my veins. I took her hand as we made our way through the villa to the lavish suite. The dim light from the setting sun streamed in through the open glass doors, bathing the luxurious room in a warm, sensual glow. Beyond the expansive terrace, ocean waves lapped gently at the white sand, the perfect rhythm for what I was about to do—almost. Just one this was missing.

With a flick of my thumb, I queued a track from my phone, and the hidden speakers came alive. "Sweet Release" by Nu Aspect spilled into the room, its deep basslines and hypnotic synths pulsing with slow, sultry energy. The music throbbed like a heartbeat, each beat steeped in temptation, wrapping around us in a haze of heat and desire. It was the kind of song that demanded surrender—dark, sexy, and impossible to ignore.

Returning my attention back to Krystina, I slowly undressed her, savoring every inch of her creamy skin. Her curves drove me wild. I could never—would never—get enough of the fiery goddess before me.

"Fuck, angel. You're so beautiful, it hurts," I growled, my voice low and gravelly as I bent down to trail hot, open-mouthed kisses along her neck and collarbone. My need for her grew hotter by the second. "And you're all mine."

"Yours," she moaned, arching her back as my tongue trailed lower, teasing her hardened nipples.

With expert precision, my wife's skilled fingers found their way to the buttons of my white shirt, urgency building in our heated tango. When she was completely naked, and I was left shirtless with only my khaki shorts, I stepped back.

"Sit down," I told her.

I watched Krystina perch on the edge of the bed, her brown curls cascading over her bare shoulders as she gazed at me with those mesmerizing chocolate eyes. A surge of emotion coursed through me at the sight of her—my wife, my soulmate, the woman who ignited a fire in my very soul.

"You're ravishing," I murmured, drinking in every exquisite detail of her.

She grinned playfully. "That's quite an old-fashioned

word. You're making me feel like Scarlet O'Hara. Will you be like Rhett Butler and throw me over your shoulder so you can have your way with me?"

Her casual flirtations never failed to stir something primal within me. She filled me with an intoxicating blend of tenderness and raw desire that I'd never experienced with anyone else. She was my anchor, my purpose, the missing piece that made this broken man whole again.

"Oh, I'll have my way with you, Mrs. Stone. Remember my only rule for this trip: I'm in control of everything at all times. But before I have my way with you, I have a wedding present for you."

"But you already gave me a present. They were the earrings I wore on our wedding day."

I moved deliberately toward my suitcase, hyperaware of her curious gaze following my every movement. "Angel, I'll never stop giving you gifts. You really need to get used to it."

Feeling around the inner pocket of my suitcase, my fingers closed around the small box nestled inside. I held up the box wrapped in shimmering silver paper and tied with a delicate bow.

"You spoil me, Alex."

I chuckled softly as I approached her, the weight of the box in my hand a reminder of its significance. This gift represented more than just a trinket. It symbolized the journey we were on together—past, present, and future.

I extended the box to Krystina, hearing her breath catch when her fingers brushed against mine. Our eyes locked, and in that silent exchange, I saw a reflection of my desire.

As she lay there naked on the bed, she carefully untied the bow, her nimble fingers working with delicate precision. The wrapping paper fell away, revealing a sleek black box beneath. She cracked it open.

"Oh!" Krystina gasped, her brown eyes widening in surprise and delight. "It's beautiful!"

She lifted the anklet from its velvet cushion, the delicate platinum chain catching the soft cabin light. The tiny triskelion key charm encrusted with diamonds dangled, spinning slowly.

I drank in her expression of wonder, committing every detail to memory—the slight parting of her lips, the sparkle in her eyes, and the way her curls framed her face as she leaned in to examine the charm more closely.

"Allow me," I said, gesturing to her ankle.

I took the anklet from her hands, my fingers brushing against hers. The contact sent goosebumps over her skin. Kneeling at her feet, I traced the delicate curve of her ankle, savoring her softness. With deliberate slowness, I fastened the clasp.

"Now," I began, kissing my way up her leg. "I believe I have unfinished business to attend to."

Her breath hitched, and I saw her eyes sparkle with dark desire. Then she began to fidget when I kissed a sensitive spot behind her knee, a habit I found irresistibly sexy for some unknown reason.

"What sort of business, sir?"

I sat back on my heels, maintaining eye contact and suppressing a groan. I loved when she turned into a sexual deviant.

"I think I need to blindfold you—force you to surrender control and let your other senses take over."

"Sensory deprivation. A favorite pastime of yours."

I leaned in, my voice low and resonant. "It's because it requires irrevocable trust. Your pleasure is my ultimate priority."

The air between us seemed to thicken. I could still hear the gentle lapping of waves on the shore, a rhythmic counterpoint to our quickening breaths. The scent of sea salt mingled with Krystina's flowery perfume, creating an intoxicating blend.

Unable to resist any longer, I crawled up her body, capturing her lips in a searing kiss. She responded with equal fervor, her hands sliding down to grip my shoulders. Our kiss deepened, a dance of tongues and teeth, each caress speaking volumes of our shared desire.

A soft moan escaped her, the vibration traveling through me and igniting every nerve ending. Our bodies pressed closer, the heat between us building.

"Alex," Krystina gasped as we parted for air. Her chest heaved, and she began to fumble with my belt buckle. "I need you."

And I needed her. Desperately. The blindfold would have to wait for round two.

I pressed my cock into the liquid heat that had gathered between her legs, stretching her with my girth. Inch by inch, I fed her my length, claiming her.

"This pussy is mine, angel. Forever."

"Yes. I'm yours," she said between pants. The sound of her ragged breathing was nearly enough to make me come. I gripped her hips, preparing for an explosive ride.

"I'm not going to hold back. I want you to take all of me."

Then I began to move. I started slow, but I wasn't gentle. I pushed in hard, her breath catching as she absorbed each stab of pleasure. I rocked into her over and over again, working her into a desperate fever. I leaned in to kiss the shell of her ear as my hips pumped, kissing down her neck and shoulders, pushing into her hot well until she began to tremble. Then, yanking her hips up, I pushed forward until the tip of my cock was pressing against her very core.

Instantly, she cried out from the pressure of me being so deep.

"Oh, God!" she gasped in shock.

And that's when I felt it. Pleasure shot through my veins as the walls of her pussy began to constrict around me. She sheathed my cock in heat, pulsing with desire. I pulled back slowly, then drove all the way home. Again and again, I impaled her with a savage rhythm, needing to feel her orgasm more than I needed my own. Her body writhed with pleasure, taking all that I could give.

"I'm going to come. Meet me there," she pleaded. Her desperation nearly broke my sanity. I was completely lost in her. In this. In the moment. I thrust hard, and she matched my movements, driving us to unbelievable heights. The pace grew erratic, more jerking and demanding. Our gazes locked, and she tightened around me. I pushed up, piercing her, and she cried out my name.

"Alex!"

"Give it to me now, angel. I want your orgasm," I demanded, my voice rough.

At my words, she exploded like a bomb, but I didn't stop moving. I continued to piston into her, my hands digging into her hips, demanding her to take it. Her back arched, and she cried out. This time, I allowed myself to fall with her.

My body went taut, straining so tight I thought I would burst apart at the seams. My orgasm hit from every direction. Rushes of white and color flashed before my eyes, dizzying and all-consuming.

Just as it always was with Krystina.

My wife.

Chapter 9

Krystina

The pristine stretch of Enchanted Isle's shoreline seemed to extend endlessly in both directions, a ribbon of powder-soft white sand that felt like silk beneath my bare feet. It was warm between my toes, and I found myself deliberately slowing my pace to savor the sensation. Palm trees lined the beach like sentinels, swayed lazily in the salty sea breeze, their slender trunks reaching skyward. The water gently lapped against the shore, producing a soothing melody harmonizing with the rustling of palms and the distant calls of seagulls.

"I didn't think it was possible, but it's even more beautiful here than our villa escape in Montego Bay. It makes me not want to return to reality," I murmured.

I paused to let my gaze sweep across the breathtaking

panorama before us. It stretched for miles, the landscape seeming almost too perfect to be real. It was as if we'd stepped into a postcard where every detail had been carefully curated for maximum enchantment.

Alexander's phone had buzzed earlier while we were exploring the island's hidden coves, and I'd caught a glimpse of his expression as he read the message—that subtle tightening around his eyes that meant business from the outside world was intruding on our honeymoon. He'd quickly tucked the device away and focused his attention back on me with that intense concentration that made me feel like the only person in his universe.

But curiosity had gotten the best of me, and I couldn't help asking who'd contacted him.

"That was Hale checking in," he'd said when I raised an eyebrow in question. "Just routine security updates. Helena's condition remains stable at the facility." His voice had carried that carefully neutral tone he used when discussing his mother, the woman whose existence had nearly destroyed our relationship before it began.

"And Justine?" I'd asked gently, knowing the topic of his sister was still a raw wound between them.

Alexander's jaw had tightened almost imperceptibly. "She's adjusting to the consequences of her choices," he'd said curtly before steering our conversation toward safer waters. The betrayal he felt over Justine's role in hiding the truth about their past still cut deep, creating a chasm between the siblings that might never fully heal.

Now, as we made our way along the shoreline, I found myself studying my husband's profile. His dark hair caught glints of bronze from the sun, and the strong line of his jaw spoke of determination and barely controlled power. Even in this tropical paradise, there was something predatory about the way he moved, as if he were constantly assessing his surroundings, cataloging potential threats or opportunities.

"You never did tell me how you discovered this place. Enchanted Isle seems like..." I pressed my lips together, trying to find the words to describe perfection "It's untouched, and seems like a closely guarded secret."

"I can't give away all my sources, angel. That would spoil future adventures," Alexander replied and flashed me an enigmatic smile that sent a delicious shiver through me. There was a promise in his words, painting images of other exotic locations and private moments stolen away from the world.

We continued to walk silently, both content to enjoy the island's serenity. After we left Montego Bay, we'd explored several Caribbean jewels—the sophisticated charm of Grand Cayman with its Seven Mile Beach, the lush volcanic hills of St. Lucia with its towering Pitons rising from emerald seas. Each destination had offered its own unique pleasures, but we'd always found ourselves drawn back to Enchanted Isle's untouched tranquility.

Here, there wasn't another soul for miles in any direction. It was our own private Eden, a place that seemed suspended in time. The island was too small and too remote for commercial development, its rocky outcroppings and coral formations making it nearly impossible for larger vessels to approach the shore safely. Even *The Lucy* couldn't get close, and we had to use a small motorboat to reach land.

I looked past the colorful reefs to see *The Lucy* proudly floating on the glimmering surface of the water. The dinghy we took to shore was just ahead, nestled in the sand. Today was our last day here, and once we pushed the little boat into the water and made our way back to the grandeur of *The Lucy*, it would signal the end of our honeymoon and the start of our journey back to reality.

While we had taken a plane to Jamaica, the boat had taken the long way, traveling from Montauk Marina in New York to the Caribbean. Unfortunately, our jobs didn't allow for a lengthy trip back home. The return would be much shorter. Once we pulled up anchor, we'd go north to Fort Lauderdale. From there, Alexander and I would catch a private plane back to New York and leave the hired crew to navigate *The Lucy* back to Lake Montauk.

The thought of returning to the demands of our regular lives sent a pang of regret through me. I wasn't ready. It had been three weeks of bliss with my new husband. Our trusted crew members had navigated the boat, sticking mainly to the control room and their private quarters, ensuring our paths would only cross if one went looking for the other. This allowed Alexander and me privacy aboard the expansive yacht. Explosive, lust-filled nights with me bound and at the mercy of my husband's every desire were followed by seemingly endless days on shore.

"I don't want this to end," I admitted, the words escaping before I could stop them. "These three weeks have been..." I searched for adequate words to describe the transformation I'd felt, the way being Alexander's wife had changed something fundamental inside me.

"Perfect," he finished, and there was something in his voice that told me he was feeling the same reluctance to return to our complicated world.

"Let's stay on the beach a little longer," I suggested. "Maybe we can catch the sunset."

"I don't want to tender back to *The Lucy* in the dark, Krystina. It's not safe. We can stay for a bit, but can't be on the beach when it dips below the horizon. You'll have to see the sunset from the main deck."

"Fair enough."

Determined to make the most of our final evening on the beach, I quickened my pace toward the dinghy. I had a surprise planned—a small celebration to mark the end of our honeymoon, even though I knew Alexander preferred to be the one making such arrangements. The risk of his displeasure only added to the excitement thrumming through my veins.

Reaching into one of the boat's storage compartments, I retrieved the beach blanket I'd hidden there earlier, along with a small Bluetooth speaker I'd managed to smuggle from the yacht. With a mischievous grin, I picked up my phone and selected a song from one of Alexander's playlists. Rihanna's "Only Girl" burst to life. The pounding beat and sultry vocals rolled out over the sand, bold and unapologetic.

As the chorus swelled into *Want you to make me feel, like I'm the only girl in the world*, my chest tightened. The lyrics weren't just music. They were everything I felt in that moment. That was what Alexander did to me. No matter the chaos of his world, no matter the shadows of his past, he made me feel like the center of it all—his focus, his possession, his everything. And here on this beach, I wanted to give that same feeling back to him.

"Alex, can you grab the cooler?"

When he didn't immediately respond, I turned to find him standing motionless, one dark eyebrow raised in an expression I knew all too well. The cooler already sat open beside him, revealing the champagne bottle and crystal flutes I'd carefully packed that morning. His hands held the evidence of my unauthorized planning, and the set of his jaw told me I was in for exactly the kind of trouble I'd been hoping for.

"Planned ahead, did you?" His voice carried that edge of authority that never failed to make my knees weak. I could already see the heat burning in his sapphire eyes beneath the stern facade.

"Perhaps," I replied with deliberate coyness, turning

my back to him as I began spreading the blanket across the white sand. I could feel his gaze tracking my every movement. I made sure to bend just a little more than necessary, giving him a full view of my thong bikini, knowing exactly how the gesture would affect him.

I'd barely had time to smooth the blanket's corners when I felt his arm snake around my waist with predatory swiftness. He pulled me back against the solid wall of his chest, and I could feel the heat radiating from his skin through the thin fabric of his linen shirt. His lips found my ear, his breath sending shivers cascading down my spine.

"Did you forget who makes the decisions here, Mrs. Stone?" The question was asked in that low, dominant tone that made my core clench with anticipation. "Did you forget that everything—every plan, every surprise, every moment of pleasure—belongs to me?"

The reminder of our dynamic sent heat pooling low in my belly. There was a time in our relationship when I would have challenged his stern reminder, but I was a fast learner. This was all part of the game with my dominant husband—and the reward for playing was always worth it. I'd learned to crave his control, to find deep satisfaction in surrendering my independence to his capable hands.

"I haven't forgotten," I whispered.

"Good," he murmured, and I felt him shift behind me, his arousal pressing against my lower back in a way that made my breath catch. "Because now I'm going to have to remind you exactly what happens when my angel thinks she can take charge."

The promise in his words sent electricity racing through my veins. I was in trouble.

Serious trouble.

And I couldn't wait to be punished.

I remained perfectly still as he stepped away, leaving me aching for his touch while anticipating whatever delicious punishment he had in mind.

The sound of a cork popping made me smile despite my supposed contrition. Trust Alexander to incorporate my unauthorized surprise into his own plans, to take control even of my small rebellion and make it serve his purposes.

"Turn around," he commanded, and I obeyed immediately, finding him standing before me like some pagan god of desire. His white linen shirt hung open in the tropical breeze, revealing the bronzed expanse of his chest that I longed to explore with my hands and lips. The champagne flute in his hand caught the sunlight, the bubbles rising through the pale liquid like tiny promises of intoxication.

"Drink," he ordered, bringing the glass to my lips with one hand while the other cupped the back of my neck in a gesture that was both tender and possessive.

I parted my lips obediently, allowing him to control the pace as the cool champagne slid across my tongue. The bubbles burst against my palate, adding to the effervescence already building in my bloodstream from his proximity, his scent, and his absolute command of the moment.

When the glass was empty, I deliberately let my tongue dart out to catch a lingering drop at the corner of my mouth, knowing the gesture would inflame him further.

"Are you planning to get me drunk so you can have your wicked way with me?" I asked with mock innocence.

Alexander's eyes darkened to the color of a storm-tossed sea, and he carelessly tossed the empty flute onto the sand where it landed with a soft thud.

"I don't need alcohol to have my way with you, angel," he said, his voice carrying dark promise. "You're already mine for the taking."

Slipping a finger under the thin strap of my coverup, he slid it down my arms until it pooled at my feet. After a few quick tugs on the strings at my neck, back, and hips, the scraps of material that made up my bathing suit fell to my feet.

Desire thundered through my veins. The uninhibited feeling of standing naked outdoors was unparalleled. I'd done it several times over the past couple of weeks, and each time was no less exhilarating. My body flushed, and wetness gathered at the apex of my thighs, wondering what he would do next.

Would he take me right here on the beach? On the

blanket, perhaps. Or maybe from behind, with me bent over the boat's edge.

The idea caused the devil on my shoulder to twirl in a happy dance.

Alexander's hands went down to my ass, kneading my bare cheeks as he pulled me closer to him. His erection pressed hard against my belly, nearly stabbing a hole through his shorts. His need was hot. So hot. I wanted to slip my hands inside his waistband and give him pleasure, but he held me tight, and there wasn't room for me to maneuver a hand between us.

Instead, I reached up and laced my fingers into his dark waves. He lowered his head to mine, coaxing my lips apart until our tongues danced in perfect harmony.

"I need to punish you for disobeying me," he growled into my mouth.

"Hmmm..."

"Bend over the edge of the boat." He stepped back, and I moved into the vulnerable position without hesitation. I shivered when I felt his hand skim up my thigh. My breath quickened, and despite the balmy air, goosebumps prickled over my skin when he spoke again. "Hang on tight to the side and spread your legs. I'll be giving you five strikes. The first will be for disobeying my orders and planning something without my consent."

I sucked in a breath and braced myself. We'd been here before, and I knew it would only be a matter of seconds before I felt the sting of his palm.

He gripped my hip securely with one hand and widened his stance. Then he let his hand fly. The crashing of the ocean waves drowned out the sound of the slap, but it was no less felt. My body vibrated, humming in the most exquisite way as I awaited my remaining spankings.

"Three more, one for each of the fluted glasses and the bottle of champagne." Alexander fired off the next three smacks in rapid succession, alternating cheeks and making each slap harder than the last. Then he leaned close to my ear and whispered, "The fifth spanking is just for my pleasure. I love seeing your ass red from my palm."

But the fifth didn't come—at least not right away.

I released a quiet hiss when I felt his finger trace the seam of my ass. Endorphins, arousal, and adrenaline created a heady feeling that was all-encompassing. He lingered over my tightest hole for a moment before continuing his exploration, stopping only to slide lower and feel how wet I was for him.

He growled his approval. "You never disappoint me, angel."

Without warning, he shoved two fingers inside me while delivering the final smack to my ass. I hadn't been ready for it, and my body lurched forward. I quickly widened my stance to keep from toppling into the boat.

Using my new position to his advantage, Alexander plunged his fingers in further, and I cried out from the pleasure. He played my body like a fiddle until I thought my strings would snap from the tension. His treatment was rough, demanding, and unyielding.

And I loved it.

He leaned forward, pressing his mouth close to my ear.

"You want to come?"

"Yes," I breathed.

I expected him to intensify his motions, but he abruptly pulled out of me instead. All the air released from my lungs in a frustrated whoosh.

"Later, angel," he informed coolly. "And only if you follow my every instruction."

Shit.

I hated when he refused me an orgasm, but I knew I'd follow his every command until I got my release. I might not get what I wanted now, but he wouldn't deny me forever.

"Okay," I whispered, desperately ignoring the ache between my legs.

"Okay, what?" he demanded.

"Okay, sir." My breath hitched as the breeze skittered over my bare nipples.

"Very good. Now, we need to start heading back to *The Lucy*. It will be dark before long," Alexander said matter-of-factly. It was as if he were oblivious to my desperate panting.

The bastard.

I looked past him to see our world had transformed

into a mesmerizing canvas of vibrant colors. The sun had dipped closer to the horizon, painting the sky with a breathtaking spectacle of orange, pink, and purple. The lower the sun got, the deeper the shades would become.

"You're right," I agreed reluctantly, my voice throaty and breathless.

Alexander lifted my naked body, cradling me to his chest by hooking his arms behind my back and knees, and lowered me into the dinghy. Releasing me, he turned to collect my discarded bathing suit and cover-up.

"Put this back on," he said and handed me the bits of material. "It will be off again soon enough, but the crew on *The Lucy* doesn't deserve a show in the meantime."

"How soon will I get to take it off again?" I teased as I tied the bathing suit strings at my neck.

Alexander's heated sapphire blues narrowed on me as he dug his feet into the sand and pushed the boat into the water.

"Not soon enough."

Chapter 10

Alexander

The breeze had kicked up a knot, tugging at my hair as I carefully secured the sleek dinghy to the side of *The Lucy*. I fastened a sturdy painter line to the bow, ensuring it was taught enough to accommodate the sea's ever-changing moods. In a sense, the rope was a lifeline connecting the small vessel to its mothership. It was a ritual I'd performed countless times but never gave it less care than the last. Knots were my forte after all—as Krystina could attest—and I tied each one with the finesse of an artist.

I threaded it through the chrome cleats mounted on *The Lucy*'s hull. My fingers found the familiar rhythm of the cleat hitch, under and around, back through in a figure-eight pattern. Once I was satisfied that the tender was secured correctly, I turned to offer my hand to

Krystina, who had been watching my maritime ritual with the kind of focused attention that stirred something possessive deep in my chest.

The setting sun had transformed the sky into a canvas of burnished gold and deep coral, its dying rays catching the wind-tossed highlights in her hair and turning her skin to warm honey. She moved with unconscious grace as she accepted my assistance, her fingers intertwining with mine as my wife stepped from the smaller craft onto *The Lucy*'s deck.

My wife.

I'd said that phrase a lot over the past few weeks. I wondered if I would ever get used to it. It carried a weight of wonder that surprised me. In the business world, I was accustomed to acquiring valuable assets—companies, properties, strategic advantages that enhanced my position and power. But Krystina wasn't an acquisition. She was a gift I'd somehow convinced the universe I deserved, despite all evidence to the contrary.

Leaning down, I pressed a kiss to the crown of her head.

"I need to talk to the crew for a moment, and then I'm going to see about getting us something to eat."

"I hadn't even realized we skipped dinner, Alex. If you'll give me a minute to get some proper clothes on, I can—"

"Clothes won't be necessary," I interjected. "Just head down to our bedroom. I'll get a light dinner together and bring it there. And angel—I want you naked and kneeling when I get there."

"But—"

I raised a hand to silence her and shook my head ever so slightly. I didn't need to say anything. My expression was enough for her to know I would not be challenged. The protest fell from her lips as understanding settled over her.

I raised my hand to lightly brush her cheek with the backs of my fingers, skimming my thumb along her jawline.

"Your trust is intoxicating. Go and wait for me. I won't be long. We need to finish what we started on the beach." My words were deliberate, loaded with implications that I could see registering in the dilation of her pupils and the slight catch in her breathing. She knew what I expected, and the anticipation that flared in her chocolate brown eyes sent a corresponding heat through my veins.

I raised my hand to her face, letting the backs of my fingers brush against her cheek with deliberate tenderness before my thumb traced the elegant line of her jaw. The gesture was soft, almost reverent, but it carried with it the weight of expectation and the promise of what was to come.

Without another word, I turned and walked toward the helm station with the confident stride that had served me well in boardrooms and business negotiations. *The Lucy*'s main deck was a testament to naval architecture at its finest—vast expanses of faultless planking complemented by custom seating areas designed to take advantage of both ocean views and social interaction.

Captain Isaac Davis stood near the helm station, his weathered hands resting on the central console as he consulted the integrated navigation and weather systems. At sixty-two, he'd spent more years on the water than most people devoted to their entire careers. His salt-and-pepper beard and deeply tanned complexion spoke of countless voyages across every major ocean on earth.

"Mr. Stone," Isaac said with the respectful nod that acknowledged both my ownership of the vessel and his professional authority as captain. There was an easy confidence about him that I appreciated—he was secure enough in his abilities to defer appropriately on matters of preference while never compromising on issues of safety or seamanship.

"Good evening, Isaac," I replied, noting the slight tension in his posture that suggested complications ahead. "I trust you're prepared to get us underway on schedule?"

"Yes, sir, though we may need to adjust our overnight positioning." He gestured toward the weather display, where satellite imagery showed a swirling mass of clouds several hundred miles to our north. The system appeared well-organized and potentially troublesome. "The weather service is tracking a tropical disturbance that's likely to bring deteriorating conditions to our planned route. Nothing catastrophic, but potentially uncomfortable if you still planned on leaving tonight."

I studied the display more closely, noting the storm's projected path, intensity, and timing. The Caribbean was notorious for its rapidly changing weather patterns, particularly during the late summer months when water temperatures and atmospheric conditions could spawn significant storms with little warning. What appeared to be perfect sailing weather could transform into something entirely different in a matter of hours.

"Hurricane potential?" I asked.

"Unlikely in the short term, sir. The sea and air temperatures aren't quite aligned for it. But it could easily bring sustained winds of twenty-five to thirty knots and seas in the six-to-eight-foot range to our area during the overnight. Not dangerous for a vessel of *The Lucy*'s capabilities, but certainly not comfortable for Mrs. Stone."

I nodded, appreciating both his professional assessment and his consideration for Krystina's comfort.

"What are your recommendations?"

"I'd suggest we reposition to the island's lee side for the night," he said, indicating the proposed anchorage on the chart display. "The land mass should provide substantial protection from both wind and wave. We can ride out the worst of the weather in relative comfort, then reassess conditions at first light."

"Agreed. Make it happen."

"Very good, sir. Will there be anything else after we get her repositioned?"

"No, Isaac. You and your crew have earned your rest. Just maintain the usual anchor watch and continue monitoring weather developments."

Isaac nodded, his response immediate and professional. Turning toward the other crew members, he began issuing orders with calm authority. Within minutes, *The Lucy* started to move through the water with the grace of a thoroughbred. Trusting my yacht was in good hands, I turned my attention to more important matters—my naked wife who was awaiting my return.

Leaving them to it, I walked across the large open deck. Away from the harsh city lights, the stars shone brightly, illuminating the sky like shimmering diamonds. They reflected on the large double glass doors that led to the salon. After sliding the door closed behind me, I moved to the small galley kitchen and opened the refrigerator. I was pleased to see Isaac had restocked everything precisely as I'd requested, making it easy for me to assemble a quick, no-cook meal.

Fresh provisions lined the shelves in careful arrangement—vegetables, artisanal cheeses aged to perfection, fruits selected for both peak flavor and elegant presentation. The wine selection had been curated specifically for this voyage, with bottles chosen to complement both the tropical setting and the romantic nature of our extended honeymoon.

I arranged tomatoes, red onion, olives, green peppers, and cucumbers on a platter. I topped it with cubed feta, seasoned oil, and vinegar dressing to complete the traditional Greek salad. Once that was finished, I prepared another nuts and a medley of fruits. Hearty crackers paired with velvety hummus and creamy tzatziki completed the simple meal. Even Vivian, my invaluable housekeeper and cook, would be impressed. It may not have been one of her seven-course spreads, but it would suffice.

I placed both platters on a serving tray, grabbed two wine glasses and a chilled bottle of Louis Jadot Le Montrachet Grand Cru 2016, and went to the primary suite. As I approached the doors, my thoughts were entirely focused on the woman waiting beyond them and the promise of an evening ahead.

Stepping into the bedroom, my breath immediately caught in my throat. I froze, completely mesmerized by the stunning woman kneeling near the foot of the bed with her arms behind her back and her knees apart. She defined the meaning of perfection. Desire gripped me, and I suppressed a groan.

She glanced up at me curiously, then quickly lowered her head in submission. The brief moment that our eyes met, I saw the silent invitation.

She knew her body belonged to me.

Chapter 11

Alexander

Tearing my eyes away from her delicate and creamy skin, I set the tray of food down on the small table in the corner and lit the candles already strategically placed around the room. The candlelight cast shadows that seemed to amplify the sizzling desire in the air.

Walking over to the settee, I picked up a coil of black nylon rope that draped over the back. Tonight, on the last night of our honeymoon, Krystina would be rendered helpless. I would own her, demanding her submission until every one of my desires was satiated.

I took off my shirt and moved to stand behind her. My eyes ran down the length of her flawless spine and settled on the curvature of her impeccable ass. A vision of those luscious hips opened to me flooded my brain.

Not yet.

I was nothing if not patient, and I knew the reward would be worth the wait. Squatting down behind her, I looped the rope around her wrists and went to work.

Sexual tension hung heavy in the air. The sensation of Krystina's wrists in my grip, the feeling of her vulnerability and trust, was intoxicating. It fueled the pure, carnal need that coursed through my veins. I watched as her hands, delicate and graceful, succumbed to my binding. As my fingers brushed against her skin, she trembled, a thrilling response to the impending restraint. There was a moment of resistance, a flicker of uncertainty before she willingly yielded to the erotic tension.

It was a dance of dominance and submission, a sensual interplay of power and trust that left us both breathless. I gripped her neck and angled her head back to look at me. Her eyes filled with a mix of anticipation and surrender. She held my gaze, and at that moment, we were bound not just by restraints but by an unspoken understanding of mutual pleasure.

I stood and moved to the stereo system. With a few quick taps, Demi Lovato's "Body Say" spilled from the speakers, low and throbbing. The sultry beat and seductive lyrics filled the air, the kind of music that demanded skin on skin, every note dripping with desire and raw hunger. It was a soundtrack made for surrender.

Once the music was set, I shifted to the table and retrieved the tray of food and drink. Selecting a succulent strawberry, I brought the crimson fruit to her mouth. With deliberate slowness, she parted her lips to accept the offering. Her teeth grazed it delicately with a hint of a knowing smile playing on her mouth.

This went on for the next thirty minutes. Each morsel I offered her, each shared bite, became an intimate exchange of desire and pleasure until I thought I might combust. I wanted her more than ever before. It was an unexplainable need of epic proportions.

I was desperate to be inside her.

To feel her velvet heat.

Pushing the tray of food to the side, I reached up with both hands and brushed the pads of my thumbs over her nipples. My touch caused them to harden into erect peaks instantly. She sucked in a tiny breath, followed by an exhale of desperation. I pinched, twisting each nipple between my thumbs and forefingers, relishing the weight of her bare breasts in my hands. When she moaned, any willpower I had to put things off any longer was thrown to the wayside.

I lowered my head and took a rigid peak into my mouth. She gasped in pleasure as I sucked and rolled it around my tongue. She tilted her head back, inviting me to take more, and I silently thanked all that was divine for gifting me this woman.

Moving up to claim her mouth, I pushed my tongue past her waiting lips and devoured her. She moaned, the vibration of her lips sending an electric shock straight to my groin. Our kiss was a dance of passion, conveying emotions that went beyond any spoken words. I worked my way down her neck, savoring the feel of her pulse hammering beneath her skin as I breathed in her scent. She smelled like coconut-kissed vanilla.

"God, Krystina. The things you make me want to do to you..."

I nipped up her neck to her earlobe. She lolled her head to the side and allowed me better access. I wrapped my arms around her and pulled her body tighter against me. She sighed her appreciation, and I crushed my mouth against hers again.

Lifting her, I wrapped those glorious legs around my waist. The heat of her sex pressed against the ridges of my abdomen. She pushed forward, grinding against me, telling me her need was hot. I could have buried my cock in her right then—to drive into her like the wild animal she made me. But she deserved more than that tonight.

My wife merited worshipping.

I set her down on the edge of the bed covered in satin, kissing down her body, over her shoulders, breasts, and thighs, savoring the delicious taste of her skin.

I spread her legs apart and pressed my cheek against her inner thigh. Her exposed lips were lush, pink, and inviting.

"Oh, angel."

My face hovered over her glistening sex, and I blew softly until she began to pant. I couldn't wait any longer. I had to taste her. I swiped my tongue over her clit. Her breath hitched, and she cried out. It was all the encouragement I needed to bury my face in her soaking wet heat.

I reached up and took hold of her breasts, gratified to feel her nipples still pebbled from arousal. I twisted and pulled at the taut peaks. The pulsing in her clit signaled she was already near release, but I kept her on edge and didn't allow her to come. Her back arched as I circled and teased, deliberately driving her to madness.

Her breath was ragged when she looked down at me, eyes wild and full of passion. Her cheeks were flushed, and her gaze was desperate.

I pushed her backward onto the bed. Her bound hands forced her back into an arch, elevating her breasts. I shoved her legs up roughly and spread her wide. Then I devoured her like a starving man who would never get his fill.

It wasn't long before she cried out. Her juices, the sweetest of all nectars, coated my tongue and lips as I suckled every drop of her release. I felt a tremble course down her legs and smiled in satisfaction.

"I've only just begun, angel."

Taking advantage of her lithe state, I removed the rest of my clothing. My cock sprang free, happy to be released. Climbing back onto the bed, I flipped her onto her stomach and straddled her hips. With experienced fingers, I quickly untied the rope that was binding her arms together. Once completely unraveled, I slid off the bed and fashioned new knots. These would be to secure her ankles to the bedposts.

Once she was secure, I looked to see if she showed any level of discomfort. Her head was angled to the side with her lips parted slightly. But her eyes—those pools of chocolate brown—were dark with want. She knew how defenseless she was in this position. Lying face down with her legs bound open, her ass and pussy were vulnerable to my every desire.

"I'm going to bury my cock inside you. Deep. You'll feel every inch of me." I paused and slid a finger over her puckered rear. "Everywhere."

Her response was a carnal moan that was music to my ears. I skimmed my hand down to part her wet slit. One finger. Two fingers. I slowly and deliberately stretched her, preparing her for my invasion. She was more than ready for me.

I positioned myself at her waiting entrance. Gripping her hips, I speared her opening, easily sliding to the hilt. Her breath caught, and her mouth went slack as she absorbed each stab of pleasure. I moved hard and fast, in and out, working her into a desperate frenzy.

"Alex, make me come. Please! I need to come around you!"

I loved it when she begged. Something about the way the word "please" sounded on her lips made me wild with lust.

I kissed the back of her neck and shoulders, then pulled up her hips until she was on her hands and knees. With her ankles still secured to the bedposts, her thighs were forced further apart. Every intimate part of her was open and more exposed to me than ever. She exhaled and closed her eyes. I groaned and pushed forward until the tip of my cock was pressing against her very core.

"Oh!" she gasped in shock.

I knew how much she liked it this way—deep from behind, with my cock hitting every internal pleasure point. White-hot pleasure rocketed through my veins as the walls of her vagina constricted to adjust to me. She wrapped me in heat, pulsing with desire.

"Come for me, Krystina."

I pulled back slowly, then drove home again. And again.

"Alex! she screamed out. Her body writhed with pleasure, her climax vibrating around my cock. But I didn't stop. I wanted more—to take and give all I could.

She was like a goddess with her head thrown back in passion—her opulent chestnut curls a wild mane around her head, and her lush breasts bouncing as I thrust into her. I gave her bottom a light smack.

"Yes! she screamed out. Again!"

Holy fuck. This woman.

"You it rough. You need to be dominated. You crave it."

I smacked her again, this time harder than the last. I pounded into her, spanking her repeatedly until her ass was bright red and my palm stung. Krystina clawed at the sheets, rocking and moaning as I possessed her. She was wild with need, and I knew she'd take anything I had to offer.

Without breaking our connection, I reached over to the nightstand and retrieved a butt plug and bottle of lube. Krystina watched me, her eyes wide with trepidation. However, we'd been here before, and she trusted me. The ultimate pleasure was only a breath away as long as she relaxed her body enough to accept it.

And that she did.

With ample lube, the plug slid in with minimal resistance until all I could see was the jeweled end. Once it was in place, her pussy clenched impossibly tighter around my cock.

"Fuuuuck," I moaned.

Then I began to move again. I pounded into her with a savagery like never before—dominating her. Owning her. She was mine, and I was hers.

For all of eternity.

I took us higher and higher until I felt her stiffen. Reaching under her, I pinched her clit just hard enough to heighten her orgasm. When her climax rocketed through her body, she screamed.

"Ahhh, Alex!"

Her sex tightened like a vice around me, and I knew I would soon follow her.

I gripped her hips and slammed into her.

"Krystina, I'm right there!" I hissed through clenched teeth.

"Let me feel it deep. Please, Alex!"

Please.

Her spectacular cry was enough to send me over the edge. My mind went blank before a bright awareness spread through me. I plunged deep and held the position, allowing my seed to erupt into the intimate recesses of her body.

My connection to the extraordinary woman beneath me was complete.

Chapter 12

Krystina

I lay there staring out the portside window, waiting to catch my breath. The moon cast a silvery glow on the water. The gentle waves seem to serenade us, their melody so enchanting I could easily drift off. Every inch of me was splendidly numb, languid, and sexually satiated.

"Oh no, Mrs. Stone. I'm not done with you yet," Alexander murmured into my ear. His body lay sprawled over my backside, with most of his weight balanced on his right side so he didn't crush me. "But first, you need to eat more. I got distracted before we could finish our meal."

As if on cue, my stomach gave a little rumble. That hour-long sex-a-thon had clearly worked off what I had eaten just a short time ago.

He moved down my body with maddening slowness, each kiss a whisper of heat against fevered skin. His mouth mapped me like sacred territory, pausing just long enough in each place to leave me aching for more before moving on. When he reached my ankles, the brush of his lips sent a shiver shooting up my spine. Deft fingers made quick work of releasing my bound ankles, the rope slipping away.

Without a word, his hands traveled back up, the warmth of his palms lingering in their wake. A firm tap on my hip—a silent command. My pulse skipped. I obeyed instantly, flipping onto my back, the mattress dipping under my weight.

He repeated his earlier handiwork, focusing once again on my wrists. Except this time, he secured them high against the headboard. The fibers kissed my skin, snug but not cruel, holding me in the perfect balance of restraint and surrender.

"I can't eat if my hands are tied up," I pointed out, my voice breathy with both protest and anticipation.

"I'll feed you."

Of course, he will. How silly of me.

I felt the corners of my mouth tilt up in a knowing smile, anxious to find out what else my husband had in store for me.

Once my wrists were anchored, he shifted me until I was propped against the pillows, loosening the ropes just enough for comfort. Then his hands framed my face, his touch both reverent and claiming, before his mouth descended on mine.

The kiss hit like a storm—hard, hungry, hot, and utterly consuming. His tongue tangled with mine in an erotic rhythm that stole my breath and made my toes curl. I melted beneath him, my body liquefying under the dominance of his touch.

Almost as suddenly as it began, he broke away, leaving me gasping in the charged air between us. He slid off the bed, only to return moments later with a tray. My curiosity spiked as he set it aside, positioning himself so my legs draped over his thighs and disappeared behind his back.

I glanced down—there he was, his thick length resting heavily on the bed between us, the sight alone sending a bolt of raw need straight through me. My throat tightened with the urge to taste him, but I swallowed it down, my body thrumming with restrained hunger.

Alexander plucked a plump, glistening olive from the tray and brought it to my lips. His sapphire eyes locked on mine, darkened with a heat that made my pulse race. Slowly, he pushed the briny fruit past my lips, his gaze daring me to take it. I chewed, the tangy burst filling my mouth, while his other hand skimmed down my throat, between my breasts, and lower still until he found the slick evidence of my desire.

He traced along my slit with deliberate precision, my body reacting instantly—tightening, clenching, the subtle pressure against the plug still nestled inside me making my breath hitch. He fed me another olive, then a bite of creamy cheese and ripe tomato, each morsel accompanied by the decadent torture of his touch.

His fingers were a concerto of pleasure—sometimes teasing, sometimes demanding—sparking heat in every nerve ending they brushed. My body trembled, awareness narrowing to nothing but the slide of his skin against mine, the electric connection between us, and the desperate, building need that threatened to consume me whole.

But he wouldn't give in to my pleas for release.

I began to lose track of time. At some point, he fashioned clamps to my nipples. The hard points protruded through the tiny vises, vulnerable and sensitive to the slightest touch. When he leaned forward to flick his tongue over an erect peak, I nearly bucked off the bed.

"Alex, please!"

I felt the curve of his smile on the side of my breast, and I wanted to scream. My need and desire were so hot it was near agony. So when he finally curled his fingers inside me, my orgasm was instantaneous.

"That's it, angel. Come for me," Alexander demanded in a gravely tone.

Air stole from my lungs, freezing me in place as the intense swell surged through me. It rose faster and hotter until I thought I was going to explode. Stars dotted my vision when Alexander plunged a third finger inside me, flexing mercilessly to prolong my orgasm. Wave after wave of pleasure rocketed through me.

"Oh...God." I could barely breathe the words as I rocked my hips, milking his fingers until the tremors began to subside. A delicious tingling extended to the tips of my every extremity.

Once I'd come down from the intense high, he removed his fingers from my body and shifted closer until we were mere inches apart. He brought his gaze to my lips, then raised his hand to place the fingers that were slick with my juices to my lips.

"Lick them clean," he ordered.

Meeting his eyes, a magnetic pull intensified our connection as I parted my lips enough for him to push his fingers into my mouth. My tangy flavor, combined with his salty release from earlier, coated my tongue, reminding me of the intensity of our connection.

Oh, wow. This is hot.

I traced over each digit in a slow, deliberate dance— my tongue curling and gliding in a rhythm meant only for him. Every movement was a silent promise, an offering, an invitation. His gaze locked on mine with an intensity that made my skin prickle, like he was memorizing not just the way I touched him, but the very essence of me.

When I suckled, his breath caught—a sharp inhale that sent a ripple of satisfaction through me. His eyes roamed, sometimes holding me captive with their piercing stare, only to drift downward, lingering on my breasts with a hunger that made me burn. I loved that look—the way it stripped me bare without a single touch, the way it told me I was his perfect vision of desire. That I was more than enough. That I was everything. The low, primal growl rumbling from his chest was all the confirmation I needed, a sound that vibrated straight through my core.

When he finally seemed satisfied, he slid his fingers from my mouth, leaving a faint trail of warmth in their wake, only to claim me with his lips. His kiss was a delicious contradiction—soft yet edged with dominance that brooked no refusal. He drew me closer, his grip unyielding as he guided me down until my back sank into the mattress. My arms stretched above my head, the restraints biting sweetly into my skin, a physical reminder of just how much control I had surrendered.

And God, how I craved it.

His body pressed down on mine, his defined edges and contracting muscles sharply opposing my soft curves. Our breaths mingled, creating a shared rhythm that mirrored the beat of our hearts. When he entered me again, the world around us faded into a dreamy cosmos, leaving only the intensity of the moment.

Chapter 13

Alexander

The early light of morning spilled through the sheer curtains of *The Lucy*'s primary suite. The rays were soft and warm against my skin. The yacht swayed despite the absence of the engine humming, a reminder that we were still anchored in the crystal waters off Enchanted Isle.

I stirred slowly, my internal clock registering the time even before I glanced at the sleek chronometer on the nightstand. Nearly seven o'clock—a time that would have found me already dressed and reviewing market reports in my New York penthouse, but here in this floating sanctuary, such rigid schedules seemed like another lifetime.

My body had adapted to this new rhythm over the past three weeks, learning to wake with the sun rather than the harsh buzz of alarm clocks and urgent phone calls. The transformation surprised me—I'd built an empire on the foundation of early morning discipline and relentless scheduling. Yet, here I was, genuinely reluctant to return to that world of constant demands.

I turned my head to see if Krystina was awake, and my breath caught.

She lay beside me, her dark curls scattered over the pillow in a wild halo, her delicate features softened by sleep. The early sun painted her skin in shades of cream and rose, and her lips were slightly parted as if she were whispering secrets to her dreams. She was the kind of beautiful that made a man want to pause time—an intoxicating mix of strength, sassiness, and a vulnerability that had wrecked me from the moment we met.

Her chest rose and fell in a slow, steady rhythm. She looked as if she were savoring some particularly pleasant dream. I found myself wondering if I featured in whatever fantasy was playing behind her closed eyelids. As had happened every morning since our wedding, I felt that profound sense of wonder that this extraordinary woman was mine. The legal documents and platinum rings were merely symbols. What we'd built together transcended any contract or ceremony.

For years, I'd been alone by choice—my life filled with work, discipline, and solitude. I'd convinced myself that independence was strength, that needing another person was weakness. But those days were now over. Krystina had shown me the difference between loneliness and solitude, between existing and truly living. She'd filled a void in my soul that I'd become so accustomed to carrying that I'd never allowed myself to feel what it meant to be whole.

Careful not to wake her, I slid from the bed and stepped into the shower. The water was brisk enough to pull me from the fog of sleep but not nearly enough to wash away the memories of the past few weeks—the feel of her nails in my skin, the taste of her moans, the way she whispered my name when she was on the brink of falling apart.

When I came back into the bedroom, Krystina was sitting up in bed. The sheet clung to her chest, barely covering the swell of her naked breasts.

"Are we still anchored?" she asked, her voice still thick from sleep.

"Yes. Why?"

"Good," she announced, exhaling sharply. She pushed back the covers with sudden determination, her movements filled with purpose. "I was afraid we'd already left. We need to go back to the island."

I frowned. "Go back? Krystina, I've already given Isaac our departure instructions. We were already delayed due to weather. It looks clear now, and the crew should be preparing to—"

"This will be quick," she interrupted, tossing the covers aside. The sheet slid away, revealing every inch of her bare skin in a torturous tease. She crossed the room without a shred of modesty, pulling a pair of panties and a light blue sundress from the closet.

The sight of her moving about the room naked sent an immediate surge of desire through me, my body responding with the same intensity that had characterized our entire honeymoon. She was grace personified—every curve and line of her form speaking to something primal and possessive within me. The morning light played across her skin, highlighting the gentle slope of her shoulders and the elegant line of her spine, making it nearly impossible to focus on whatever urgent mission had captured her attention.

My gaze tracked up those legs—endless, toned, and still marked faintly from my hands the night before. Without conscious thought, I crossed the cabin in three quick strides, my hands finding her waist and pulling her back against my chest. The sundress slipped from her fingers to the floor.

"Alex!" she gasped, laughing as I buried my mouth in the curve of her neck, tasting the faint sweetness of her skin.

"I need to feel you," I growled against the sensitive skin of her throat, my lips finding the spot that never failed to make her knees weak. "The way you look right now... It's taking every ounce of my control not to carry you back to that bed and have a repeat of last night."

"You are insatiable." She wriggled in my arms, her laughter breathless but her pulse racing under my lips.

"Later. Many times, if you want. It's going to be a long trip back to the mainland. I just need to do this one thing first. Please, Alex. It's important."

Reluctantly, I loosened my hold. She bent to retrieve the dress, and the moment that soft cotton hid her body, I felt the loss like a physical ache.

"I think you've forgotten the rules again, Krystina. I'm in charge, remember?"

"Yeah, yeah, Mr. Bossy Pants," she replied with an airy wave of her hand that would have earned a much stronger response under different circumstances. She disappeared into the bathroom, and I could hear the sound of water running. When she emerged, her curls were tamed into some semblance of order, and her face glowed with a natural beauty that expensive cosmetics could never replicate.

"Mr. Bossy Pants, huh?" I echoed, arching a brow.

"I need tools," she said matter-of-factly.

I blinked. "Tools?"

She tapped her chin as if deep in thought. "I'm not sure what yet. I'll know when I see them. Do you have a toolbox on board?"

"There's a large chest behind the helm."

"Perfect."

And with that, she was off like a shot.

I followed in her wake, my curiosity now thoroughly piqued. When we reached the main deck, I watched my wife approach Isaac with the kind of animated enthusiasm usually reserved for children on Christmas morning. She pointed toward the island, her hands moving in grand arcs, her laughter carrying across the waves. I was perfectly content to watch from a distance. When Krystina became overly excited about something, it was usually quite entertaining to watch.

Isaac's weathered face showed the kind of patient confusion that came from decades of dealing with the sometimes incomprehensible requests of yacht owners and their guests. He nodded appropriately and gestured toward the secured equipment locker. A few moments later, Krystina returned to me with a small canvas bag looking like trouble wrapped in sunshine. I could hear metal clanking inside.

"What's in the bag?" I asked.

She winked and replied, "You'll see."

The anticipation radiating from her was almost tangible, and her excitement was utterly contagious. Despite my natural inclination toward control and advanced planning, I found myself genuinely eager to discover whatever scheme she'd concocted.

"Lead the way, Mrs. Stone," I said, gesturing toward the dinghy that would carry us back to our private island paradise one final time.

The journey to shore was brief but filled with the kind of anticipatory tension that made every moment feel charged with significance. Krystina sat opposite me in the small tender, her tool bag clutched protectively in her lap, her eyes fixed on the approaching shoreline. When we arrived on the beach, the water gave way to the soft, powdery sand that stretched endlessly before us. The salty breeze tousled Krystina's hair as I took her hand and helped her out of the small boat.

"Now, tell me what this is all about," I demanded, but my words carried no heat. She had my complete attention now.

"Do you remember the first day you brought me to this island?"

"Of course." The corners of my mouth tilted up from the memory. "We arrived in the morning and had a picnic breakfast that we never finished because I decided a nearby boulder was the perfect place to give you a spanking."

"Exactly." She flushed, her memory obviously matching mine, but her eyes held mine steadily. "That boulder—it's where we christened this island as ours. It's where our story on Enchanted Isle began. And I need to find it again."

My brows raised, and I lashed her a devilish grin as my imagination immediately conjured several interesting possibilities for why she might want to revisit that particular location.

"Are you perhaps hoping for a repeat performance, Mrs. Stone?"

Her laughter rang out across the empty beach, pure and joyful.

"No! Well, not right now, anyway. I have something else in mind. Something that will last long after we're gone from here. Do you recall the location?"

"I do. It's this way."

With her hand firmly clasped in mine, I led her down the shore toward the secluded area she was referring to.

"Look, there it is!" The energy in her voice matched the sparkle in her eyes.

I followed her gaze and saw the massive boulder standing sentinel on the beach, bathed in the shadows of the surrounding palm trees. Looking at it now, I could almost feel the phantom sting in my palm from the morning when I'd reddened her perfect bottom until she'd begged me to stop. The memory sent a familiar surge of heat through me, along with a dozen other recollections of the ways we'd claimed this space as our own over the weeks that followed.

I'd picked this location deliberately, far out of sight from any crew member on *The Lucy*, knowing I could strip Krystina bare and fuck her into oblivion.

And that was exactly what I'd done.

"Yes, Krystina. That's the place. Now, I've been patient with this unexpected excursion so far. It's time for you to tell me why you dragged us back here," I demanded, my voice laced with authority. If she held out much longer, she would be getting that spanking whether she wanted it or not.

She closed the remaining distance to the boulder, her steps purposeful.

"I want to leave our mark here," she said, setting down her tool bag and reaching inside. "Something permanent."

When she procured chiseling tools, I raised a curious brow.

"Do I dare ask what those are for?"

She didn't answer immediately. Instead, she approached the boulder's smoothest face, running her hands over the granite surface with the concentration of a sculptor selecting marble. When she found the spot that satisfied her artistic vision, she positioned the chisel with mathematical precision and raised the hammer.

The first strike rang out across the empty beach like a bell, the metallic percussion echoing, cutting through the calls of seagulls flying overhead and the distant crash of waves. Then another strike, and another, as she began working with a determination that was both impressive and profoundly moving.

I watched, transfixed, as her intentions became clear. She was etching our initials into the hard surface. I brought my attention back to her face, a slight smile forming when I saw the determined set to her jaw. Her movements were deliberate, the stone seeming to surrender willingly to her efforts.

A profound sense of longing washed over me as I watched her. At that moment, I yearned to be closer to her, to somehow share in this intimate act of creation. She was a vision, a woman who commanded both admiration and desire, not only for her physical beauty but also for the depth of her character. The grace with which she etched our love made my heart constrict.

"You are incredible, angel. Do you know that?"

She paused her chiseling, frowning as she studied the carving thus far.

"Incredible isn't how I would describe this. I'm just hoping for legible," Krystina said with a laugh.

"I'm not talking about your artistic abilities, but for everything you are—the way you see the world, the way you find magic in moments that other people would simply let pass." I paused, my words to describe the woman before suddenly seeming inadequate. "You've made my life richer than I ever thought possible."

She looked away from her work, her chocolate brown eyes meeting mine.

"You're the love of my life, Alex. "This carving is more than just our initials. It's a symbol of everything we've built together, everything we've survived, everything we've become. It's something that will endure long after we're gone. The evidence of our love will be etched in stone forever."

The words hit me with unexpected force, resonating through my chest with the kind of emotional impact I'd only ever feel with Krystina. She was creating more than just a carving—she was establishing a monument to our connection, a permanent testament to the bond we'd forged in this paradise setting.

I pulled her into my arms, and a tender smile graced her lips. It was a smile that held a thousand unspoken words—a smile that spoke of shared memories, trials, and triumphs.

"Forever, you say?"

"Forever," she confirmed. Pressing up on her toes, she brushed her lips softly over mine. "Because forever we will be."

As the sun rose on the horizon, bringing with it a new day, I felt her words in the depths of my soul. We shared a moment of silence, basking in the memories that this place held for us. Our honeymoon might be ending, but what we'd built here—what she had literally etched into stone—would endure.

Forever with my angel was not just beginning. It was being made permanent, one careful strike of the hammer at a time.

Thank you for reading ETCHED IN STONE! I hope you enjoyed Krystina and Alexander's honeymoon. Wishing Stone is the next book in their saga.

Need to start at the beginning?
Here's the reading order:

ABOUT THE STONE SAGA

Krystina

I'm flawed and damaged. My capacity for love is limited, and I know I'm the only one who can repair the pieces of my shattered heart.

But that was before meeting Alexander Stone.

Now, he is everywhere I turn—in my mind, in my heart, and in my soul. I can't deny him. He's the glue holding my soul together. He's my addiction, and I'm unable to stay away.

But committing to love Alexander is only the beginning. When he's blackmailed about a secret he's kept since childhood, everything we fought to overcome is threatened, rocking the fragile foundation our relationship is built upon—trust.

Alexander

I had rules. Krystina broke them.

She's strong, determined, devastatingly beautiful—and stubborn as hell. Her quick wit and firecracker attitude is the complete opposite of what I want in a woman.

But I still want to claim her, tame her, and make her mine. And I always get what I want.

However, being with someone like her is a risk.

I have too many secrets. Surrendering the truth would be devastating—not only to the empire that I worked so hard to build, but to my very identity.

This 5-book series follows the same couple throughout. It's a steamy romantic suspense with dark themes, including kidnapping, blackmail, death, and complicated family dynamics.

Welcome to the Shameless Billionaire Club. Guaranteed to be a little dark, twisted, and very shameless.

➤ Start reading: https://geni.us/AuKu

MUSIC PLAYLIST FOR ETCHED IN STONE

Thank you to the musical talents who influenced and inspired *Etched In Stone*. Their creativity helped me bring Krystina and Alexander's honeymoon to life.

Listen on Spotify!

"Adore You" by Harry Styles
"Your Lovin' is Enough" by Pana, Likkle Jordee
"Do Anything" by Lion Rezz
"Sweet Release" by Nu Aspect
"Only Girl (In the World)" by Rihanna
"Body Say" by Demi Lovato

SUBSCRIBE TO DAKOTA'S NEWSLETTER

My newsletter goes out once per week with the occasional sale notice in between. It's packed with new content, sales on signed paperbacks and bookish merchandise from my online store, and giveaways. Don't miss out!

SUBSCRIBE HERE: https://dakotawillink.com/subscribe

BOOKS & BOXED WINE CONFESSIONS

Want fun stuff and sneak peek excerpts from Dakota? Join Books & Boxed Wine Confessions and get the inside scoop! Fans in this interactive reader Facebook group are the first to know the latest news!

JOIN HERE: https://www.facebook.com/groups/1635080436793794

ABOUT THE AUTHOR

Dakota Willink is an award-winning *USA Today* Bestselling Author from New York. She loves writing about damaged heroes who fall in love with sassy and independent females. Her books are character-driven, emotional, and sexy, yet written with a flare that keeps them real. With a wide range of publications, Dakota's imagination is constantly spinning new ideas. Her work has been translated into six languages and she has sold over 1 million books worldwide.

Dakota often says she survived her first publishing with coffee and wine. She's an unabashed *Star Wars* fanatic and still dreams of getting her letter from Hogwarts one day. Her daily routines usually include rocking Lululemon yoga pants, putting on lipstick, and obsessing over Excel spreadsheets. Two spoiled Cavaliers are her furry writing companions who bring her regular smiles. She enjoys traveling with her husband and debating social and economic issues with her politically savvy Generation Z son and daughter.

Dakota's favorite book genres include contemporary or dark romance, political & psychological thrillers, and autobiographies.

☘

AWARDS, ACCOLADES, AND OTHER PROJECTS

The Stone Saga is Dakota's first published book series. It has been recognized for various awards and bestseller lists, including *USA Today* and the *Readers' Favorite* 2017 Gold Medal in Romance, and has since been translated into multiple languages internationally.

The *Fade Into You* series (formally known as the *Cadence* duet) was a finalist in the *HEAR Now Festival Independent Audiobook Awards*.

In addition, Dakota has written under the alternate pen name, Marie Christy. Under this name, she has written and published a children's book for charity titled, *And I Smile*.

Also writing as Marie Christy, she was a contributor to the Blunder Woman Productions project, *Nevertheless We Persisted: Me Too*, a 2019 *Audie Award Finalist* and *Earphones Awards Winner*. This project inspired Dakota to write *The Sound of Silence*, a dark romantic suspense novel that tackles the realities of domestic abuse.

Dakota Willink is the founder of Dragonfly Ink Publishing, whose mission is to promote a common passion for reading by partnering with like-minded authors and industry professionals. Through this company, Dakota created the *Love & Lace Inkorporated*

Magazine and the *Leave Me Breathless World*, hosted ALLURE Audiobook Con, and sponsored various charity anthologies.

Printed in Dunstable, United Kingdom